Rashid's piercing blue eyes burned through her. The heavy scent of roses, the bitter taste of coffee in her mouth, the feel of heat surrounding her all combined. Polly watched, fixed like a rabbit in headlights, as Rashid drank his coffee.

She noticed the movement of his throat as he swallowed. Noticed the way his hand held the cup. Strong, beautiful hands. The kind of hands you would want to caress your body. And then her eyes travelled up to his lips. The kind of lips you would *want* to kiss you.

This was fantasy. She didn't know him. Knew very little about him, even. He wasn't and couldn't ever be part of her world, but what she was feeling was as old as time itself. She knew it, even though it frightened her.

Dear Reader

There is something so dangerous about a sheikh. The ultimate fantasy hero, perhaps? Strong, charismatic, and the ruler of all he surveys. I love them.

You won't be surprised to learn that I couldn't resist the opportunity to create my own slice of Arabia, particularly since my dad spent much of his working life building hospitals and schools across the Middle East. My brother and I grew up with his tales of meeting sheikhs in their sumptuous homes and descriptions of shopping in the souk.

Think modern cities, exotic palaces steeped in history, dunes shaped by the wind to create a starkly beautiful desert landscape and you will have caught a glimpse of the Kingdom of Amrah. Now think of two powerful men, and imagine what kind of women might stop them in their tracks and change them for the better.

The Brides of Amrah Kingdom duet begins here, with Rashid's story. Loyal and fiercely protective of those he loves, he's a man who yearns for acceptance. Polly might be a twenty-first century 'Cinderella' but she does the saving.

And then there's Hanif. Serious, dutiful, and the man who will be King of Amrah...

He needs a bride he really doesn't expect! Remember Princess Isabella of Andovaria, Seb's irresponsible sister from CROWNED: AN ORDINARY GIRL? I think she'll be just perfect.

With love

Natasha

CINDERELLA AND THE SHEIKH

BY
NATASHA OAKLEY

MILLS & BOON®
Pure reading pleasure™

First published in Great Britain 2008
Harlequin Mills & Boon Limited,
Eton House, 18-24 Paradise Road, Richmond, Surrey TW9 1SR

© Natasha Oakley 2008

ISBN: 978 0 263 20391 2

Natasha Oakley told everyone at her primary school that she wanted to be an author when she grew up. Her plan was to stay at home and have her mum bring her coffee at regular intervals—a drink she didn't like then. The coffee addiction became reality, and the love of storytelling stayed with her. A professional actress, Natasha began writing when her fifth child started to sleep through the night. Born in London, she now lives in Bedfordshire with her husband and young family. When not writing, or needed for 'crowd control', she loves to escape to antiques fairs and auctions. Find out more about Natasha and her books on her website www.natashaoakley.com

'One of the best writers
of contemporary romance writing today!'
—*cataromance.com*

THE BRIDES OF AMRAH KINGDOM
Don't miss the future King of Amrah's story
Coming soon!

For my Dad

CHAPTER ONE

'SHOULD I know him?' Polly Anderson pulled the A4 photograph across the table so she could see it more clearly. She squinted down at it, trying to bring it into focus.

Her friend smiled. 'Forget your contact lenses this morning?'

'I didn't forget them.' Polly accepted the black coffee Minty handed her and took a quick sip of the scalding liquid. 'It was a late night and my eyes feel like they're filled with grit if you really want to know.'

'And you're too vain to wear your glasses, of course.'

Polly grimaced. More that she'd put them down somewhere and had absolutely no idea where. She set the blue and white mug down on the table. 'I'm sure I've not met him. He's not exactly in the usual run of sheikhs that do business with Anthony, you know.'

'Not fat or old.'

'Something like that.'

Minty laughed her husky laugh and slid a second photograph along the table. 'You should see him without the headscarf. Then we just get tall, dark and deliciously dangerous.'

'Nice,' Polly said, looking down at the image of an

aggressively handsome man. Actually *very* nice. Her sight wasn't so short she couldn't see that. It was all about the eyes, she decided. *Mostly about the eyes.* Unexpectedly blue in a face that was unmistakably Arab.

Exotic and familiar at the same time. And incredibly sexy. Those eyes seemed to promise feelings and sensations she'd no experience of. Or very little.

She smiled. Maybe there was more of her scandalous great-great-grandmother in her than she'd supposed. Now *that* was an interesting thought—and probably one her mother would prefer her not to dwell on. 'So, who is he?' she asked, looking up.

'Officially, His Highness Prince Rashid bin Khalid bin Abdullah Al Baha. But for Western consumption he's generally known as Sheikh Rashid Al Baha. Much simpler. Twenty-nine. Six feet two and a half inches. Single. Keen horseman. Rich beyond your wildest dreams.' Minty leant forward. 'Pretty damn sexy all round.'

Polly laughed. 'Not that you're interested or anything.'

'Actually I'm not. He's a bad idea as anything other than eye candy. He's Crown Prince Khalid's second son. The one he had with his English wife—'

'Oh, okay…I've heard of him,' Polly interrupted. 'He's Amrah's playboy sheikh, right?'

Minty nodded. 'That's him. Plays hard and fast. Only thing he really exhibits any sort of commitment to is his horses. I don't understand all that, but he's something big in the horse world. Breeds them or something. Which is why I thought you might have met him through that slimy stepbrother of yours. But if not it doesn't really matter. We'll manage.'

Polly picked up the more traditional of the two pictures and held it out in front of her. Long flowing white robes and his dark hair concealed beneath a white headdress.

Minty was right. Prince Rashid bin thingy was really very sexy. If he'd been to Shelton she'd have remembered.

She closed one eyelid to focus more clearly. 'A couple of sheikhs did come over from Amrah but they were both much older. And I doubt they were royalty because Anthony would have been much more impressed. I can probably get their names for you if you need them.'

Minty shook her head and bent over to open the file resting against the leg of her chair. 'I don't. But while we're at it, have a look at his elder brother,' she said, passing across another glossy A4 picture. 'His Highness Prince Hanif bin Khalid bin Abdullah Al Baha. Again he tends to contract all that to Sheikh Hanif Al Baha. And who can blame him?'

Polly picked up the photograph.

'Now their daddy's so ill Hanif's probably the one we should be talking to,' Minty said slowly, her eyes focused on her notes. 'They've both got the "bin Khalid bin Abdullah Al Baha". Exactly the same. Not very imaginative, is it? The only difference is the Hanif-Rashid bit.'

There was more difference between the brothers than that. Sheikh Hanif looked like a 'safe pair of hands'. At least, he did as far as you could ever judge anything from a single photo when you weren't wearing your glasses.

Polly closed one eyelid and brought the blurry image into sharp focus again. He had a solid sort of responsibility. Maybe a hint of sadness in his dark eyes? Certainly steeliness.

But Rashid was something else. There was a restlessness about him. A man who exuded an edginess. Danger. As Minty said, a *bad* idea. Unquestionably. Why *were* bad boys always so attractive?

'Neither of them have been to Shelton. I'm sure.

They're both a good twenty years younger than the men I met.'

Minty flicked through the pages of her notebook. 'I can't get my head round these names at all. The dad is Crown Prince Khalid bin Abdullah bin Abdul-Aalee Al Baha. *Jeez.*'

'"Bin" means "son of",' Polly said, putting the photographs down and picking up her coffee. She wrapped her fingers round the comforting warmth and blew across the top of the mug. 'Think of it like a family tree. And Baha is King Abdullah's family name so that pinpoints them as being close to the centre of things.'

'That makes it all as clear as mud.' Minty rubbed at her forehead. 'Not that it matters. I think as long as you cover your shoulders and don't wear miniskirts while in Amrah we'll be just fine even if we don't get all that sorted.'

'Right.' Polly stretched out long legs encased in the finest ten-denier stockings. 'I can manage that. Seems a bit of a pity to hide my best feature, though, don't you think?'

'Better than getting arrested for immorality in a public place.'

'Do they do that?'

'I've absolutely no idea. Let's not risk it.' Then as she caught the edge of Polly's startled gaze, 'Don't let it worry you. I've got a team working on the practical side of things. Nothing horrible will happen to you, I promise.'

Polly nodded, only partially reassured.

'And Matthew Wriggley, the tame historian we found, is painstakingly putting together some wonderful detail on your Elizabeth Lewis. Really exciting. You'll love it.' She gathered the photographs together and put them inside her slip file. 'It was all going great until Crown

Prince Khalid fell ill and the permission to begin filming was mired in red tape.'

Polly said nothing. She took another sip of her coffee and waited. She'd known Minty for something like nine years and she knew there was more to come.

'So now I need you to cultivate Sheikh Rashid, get his support and encourage him to fast-track it all or we'll miss the best of the weather. Convince him we don't have any kind of subversive agenda.'

Two frown lines appeared in the centre of Polly's forehead. 'I thought you said we needed to negotiate with the elder brother now Crown Prince Khalid is ill.'

'I knew you weren't paying attention to me. Sheikh Hanif is the brother we *should* be talking to since he's generally thought to be his father's right-hand man, but he's completely un-get-able-at.'

'That's not a word.'

'You know what I mean,' Minty said, ripping the top off a sachet of artificial sweetener and dropping the contents in her coffee. 'He's doing the bedside vigil thing. Which leaves us with Sheikh Rashid—'

'Ah.'

'—who isn't, and who *fortunately* has a well-documented soft spot for English blondes.'

'How fortuitous,' Polly said dryly.

'Isn't it? Even better is that he's going to be at your place for the big charity bash this weekend. I've no idea why he isn't also sitting at his father's bedside but that's not important—'

Polly shook her head. That couldn't be right. 'His name isn't on the guest list,' she said with the quiet certainty of someone who'd been through it twice last week.

'He is. He's in the Duke of Aylesbury's party. Part of the "plus six".'

'How the *heck* do you know that when I don't?'

'One very boring dinner party sat next to an inebriated old Etonian and hey presto. It's all in the flirting.' Minty picked up her spoon and stirred her coffee. 'Apparently big brother Hanif was at Eton with the Duke of Aylesbury and they're close friends. Presumably that friendship has extended to little brother, too, I don't know. Whatever the reason, he'll be at Shelton on Saturday.'

Polly sat back in her chair and gazed in frank admiration.

'So, if you do your "charming lady of the castle" thing and get his support that should speed everything up beautifully. We've had all the appropriate forms in now for about four months—'

'Do my what?'

Minty looked up and laughed. 'You know what I mean. Foreigners love that stuff. Take him to see the Rembrandt or something. Talk about your mother the dowager duchess. Toss your hair a bit. Don't mention you're more the Cinderella of the outfit. He'll love it.' Distracted, she glanced over her shoulder, then back at Polly. 'What *is* that noise?'

'*Aargh!* That's my phone. Sorry.' Polly made a dive for her handbag. 'I should have switched it off.' The handle caught on her chair arm and by the time she'd opened her bag the ringing had stopped.

'Important?'

Polly glanced down at the number. 'Probably not. It's Anthony.' She turned it off and returned the phone to the depths of her bag. 'I'll call him later.'

'Good plan! Let him sort out the latest crisis. It's about *bloody* time he did something.'

Polly allowed herself a tiny smile. Loyalty to her late stepfather meant she always stopped short of joining in criticism of Anthony.

'How long is it now since Richard died?' Minty asked suddenly.

'Three years. Almost. It'll be three years in May.' Was it really that long? Polly replaced her bag back on the floor and picked up her coffee once again. In another four months her mother would have been widowed longer than she'd been married. Unbelievable. So much had happened.

'Plenty of time for him to have got used to the idea of running the show—'

If only. Anthony still showed absolutely no inclination to do anything of the sort.

'And if his well-bred wife thought of something other than horses that'd help.'

'They'll have to manage while I'm away filming—'

'*If* we get our permit.'

'*If,*' Polly agreed mildly.

'Well, try to sound like you mind one way or the other!'

'I do.' Her smiled twisted. *Sort of.* It was just…leaving Shelton was going to be difficult, particularly since she knew it wasn't in safe hands. Every time she tried to imagine herself packing her case and walking away from it…she couldn't.

Instead she'd think about how much there was to do. The Burns Night Supper, for example, or the Valentine's Ball, or the craft fair held at the castle each Easter weekend…

All bringing in desperately needed revenue if the conservation programme was to continue. The trouble was she *cared*. Somehow, and she didn't really understand how, it had got into her bones. Shelton Castle had become her raison d'être.

And, the truth was, it wasn't hers to love. It was Anthony's. *His* birthright. *His* privilege to nurture and succour the castle for future generations. And if she didn't manage to detach herself she would eventually be left with nothing.

Minty watched her with narrowed eyes. 'We agreed. It's time you left Shelton.'

They had agreed that.

'And way past time you did a job for which you're being properly paid.'

Also true. Her head agreed. It was her heart that was more difficult to control.

'You've got no savings, no pension, no career structure—'

'I know.' *And she did.* It wasn't something that kept her awake at night, but she did know she'd allowed herself to drift for too long.

And she knew Amrah could be the answer. The first real attempt she'd made to cut the umbilical cord that tied her to the castle.

'Well, then, be nice to Sheikh Rashid and I'll have you on a plane within twenty-four hours of getting the paperwork through.'

'Be nice to Sheikh Rashid.' That was easier said than done. There was no getting near the man. Polly moved back to conceal herself behind an extravagant white floral display of alstromeria, lisianthus and roses so she could watch him more easily. Or, more accurately, so she could watch him without anyone noticing that was what she was doing.

Sheikh Rashid sat facing out across the ballroom. As he'd done all evening. His long legs stretched out in front of him, a look of faint boredom on his face. Silent. Arrogant. And rude, if she was honest.

From the very first moment he'd arrived he'd been

permanently surrounded by women who looked as if they'd stepped out of a Bond movie, but they could have been invisible for all the attention he paid them. Perhaps he was so used to it he didn't notice they were there?

But it was rude all the same. And, speaking as someone who'd often been all but invisible, she didn't like it.

Of course, they should have moved away rather than continue to try to attract his attention. That would have been classier, but they didn't. *Of course they didn't.* They hovered about, smiling and laughing. Hoping he might notice them.

All of which made Minty's cunning plan just that little bit more difficult to bring to fulfilment and left Polly stuck behind a large floral arrangement completely uncertain what to do next.

Polly bit her lip. Minty would have powered her way across the ballroom and flicked aside all competition like flies off a trifle, but she wasn't Minty.

And he wasn't the kind of man she'd ever be comfortable approaching. Contact lenses in, she was able to confirm her initial assessment of His Highness Prince Rashid bin Khalid bin Abdullah Al Baha as sex on legs. Or would be, if you liked that kind of thing. Which she didn't.

He was all too much. Too tall. Too handsome. Too... powerful. He looked like the kind of man who could crack a nut with his bare hands and wouldn't hesitate to do the same to people if he had to. And, from all she'd read, he came from a long line of men who'd had to. Centuries of tribal disputes, years of colonial occupation and violent coups had shaped Amrah into the country it was. They'd shaped the men who ruled it, too.

It was strange to think her great-great-grandmother had been an active participant in all that history. Or a small slice of it at least.

'Something wrong?'

Polly turned to look down at her mother. 'No. Why?'

'You're frowning. I wondered if the ice sculpture was melting or the fireworks had got damp,' she said, bringing her wheelchair into line. 'It's not often I see you frowning.'

'Nothing like that. As far as I know.' Polly smiled and set her glass of untouched champagne down on the window sill behind her. 'But I ought to stop standing about and check.'

'Polly—'

She stopped.

'I just wanted to say you've done a beautiful job tonight. Again.' Her mother reached out and lightly touched her hand. 'I know Anthony doesn't appreciate the work that goes into something like this, but I do.'

'I know.' Polly spontaneously bent down and placed a kiss on her mother's cheek. 'Have you got everything you need? Can I get you a drink?'

The dowager duchess laughed. 'I'm fine. Any more champagne and I'll be arrested for being drunk in charge of a wheelchair. You do what you need to do, darling.'

'Get someone to come and find me if you want to go to bed,' she said, taking in her mother's tired face. 'There's no need for you—'

'Stop fussing. I'll be fine.' Then, her attention snagged, 'Who's that man? I don't recognise him.'

Polly followed the direction of her mother's eyes.

'With the Duke of Aylesbury? Front table, beneath the Mad Duchess oil painting?'

'That's—' She stopped as Rashid's eyes met hers. The sensation was akin to how she imagined it would feel if you stuck a wet finger into an electrical socket. He was quite, quite still…and, *heaven help her,* he was definitely watching her.

What was more he'd probably seen her watching him. Polly straightened her spine and summoned up her 'perfect hostess' smile, resisting the temptation to check that her hair was still firmly pinned in its chignon. Then, abruptly, he leant forward and spoke to the Duke of Aylesbury sitting immediately to his left.

She forced her chin that little bit higher as Sheikh Rashid's blue eyes locked with hers once more. It had to be pure imagination that made her stomach clench in…

God only knew what. The word that had sprung into her mind had been *fear*. Except that didn't make any sense.

'He looks so angry.'

'That's His Highness Prince Rashid bin Khalid bin Abdullah Al Baha.' His formal title came easily from her lips, absolutely no trace of the uneasiness she felt appearing in her voice. She dragged her eyes away. 'Why do you think he's angry?'

'I just did,' her mother said slowly, and then smiled. 'For a moment. He has a very uncompromising face.'

That was one way of putting it. It seemed to Polly he had an uncompromising everything.

Her mother released the brake on her wheelchair, apparently having lost interest. 'I hope Anthony isn't intending to do business with him. I don't think that would be a good idea at all.'

On that slightly obscure observation the dowager duchess moved away, her gloved hands moving lightly on the wheels of her chair. Polly watched her for the shortest of moments and then, deliberately not looking back at the Amrahi prince, walked towards the Long Gallery.

Or tried to. Every step she felt as though his eyes were boring into her back. All of a sudden it became difficult to walk in a straight line. She felt conscious of how her arms swung in relation to her legs. Wondered what would be the best thing to do with her hands. She hadn't felt so self-conscious since she'd left puberty.

Polly slipped out into the Long Gallery and pulled the door shut behind her with a satisfying click. She rubbed a hand over the goose bumps on her forearm. What was the matter with her? Surely if she'd learnt one thing in the last six years it was not to let these people get to her. They could look down their long patrician noses any which way they wanted. It didn't touch her. Couldn't, if she didn't let it.

But…

Still the words she needed to put a frame around what she was feeling eluded her. There was *something*. Something she couldn't quite catch at.

Call it feminine intuition, but she was certain the mind behind those blue eyes wasn't thinking about anything as pleasant as her state-school education and her mother's temerity to marry 'out of her class'.

Polly frowned. The way he'd looked at her had felt personal. He'd looked at her as though she were…

Damn it! What *was* the word?

He'd looked at her as if she were the…*enemy*. That was it. As though it were only the finest of veneers layered over his anger.

Polly shook her head. She was being ridiculous. The dark hair, olive skin, blue-eyed combination had really done something peculiar to her common sense. She didn't know him. Didn't even know very much about him and he'd have to know even less about her.

At best she'd be a name on their application for permission to film in Amrah. Maybe he just wasn't keen on a film crew coming to his country? But that hardly made sense because he could say 'no' and Minty would have to move on to another project. It was hardly something he needed to lose any sleep over.

But she might. Polly walked the length of the Long Gallery and through into the library with the wonderful smell of leather, polish and really old books. If Sheikh Rashid *did* veto the project, what would she do then? It was past time she left this place and it wasn't as though she had alternatives leaping out at her.

'Everything all right, Miss Polly?'

Polly spun round and smiled up at her stepbrother's elderly butler who'd come through the Summer Sitting Room. 'Fine. I'm just on my way to check everything's ready for the fireworks.'

'You'll find the two gentlemen from "Creative Show" in the staff room,' the butler said, the merest flicker in his eyes communicating how annoying he'd found them.

Polly smiled and gathered up the folds of her peacock-blue dress. 'We're nearly done. And the rain seems to be holding off all right so I think we'll revert to midnight. Let's get this over as soon as possible and send these people home.'

'Very good, Miss Polly.'

Miss Polly. She liked that. Henry Phillips had managed to find the perfect solution as to what to call someone who was almost one of the family but not quite.

No, not quite. She would always be the housekeeper's daughter even if her mother had married the fourteenth duke. And Henry Phillips would always remember he'd taken her into the kitchens and made her hot milk and sugar during her father's wake. It was a bond between them that would never be broken even if she was *almost* 'a member of the family'.

'Henry…?' She stopped him as a new thought occurred to her. 'What do you know about Sheikh Rashid
Al Baha? He's not been to Shelton before tonight, has
he?'

'No,' the butler answered with one of his rare smiles, 'but
I fancy he's the money who bought Golden Mile all the
same.'

'By himself?'

'Indeed.'

'He must be worth billions!'

'A little more than that,' the butler said with another
thin smile. 'I doubt it was pocket change, but nothing that
need worry him, I gather.'

'So why didn't he come here?' she asked with a frown.

'I imagine all the negotiations were carried out
through his agent. His Grace and the anonymous buyer
of Golden Mile both wished the transaction to be
private.'

'Oh.'

'Why do you ask?'

'No reason.' *Almost no reason.* It had suddenly
occurred to her that the look in Rashid Al Baha's cold blue
eyes might have had something to do with Anthony after
all. Her stepbrother made enemies easier than anyone she
knew.

'And they met tonight?'

Henry nodded.

'What happened? Did they argue?'

'That would be very unusual for someone from his
culture, I believe. They spoke and it was extremely
cordial. But—' the elderly man searched for the correct
word '—it was…shall we say, cold.'

Why? An Amrahi prince with the reputation and dis-
posable income of this one would normally have Anthony

exerting himself to charm. And even she had to own he was good at that when he saw a reason to be.

But 'cold' was exactly the word to describe the way Rashid Al Baha had looked at her earlier. Cold, angry and speculative.

CHAPTER TWO

RASHID watched the Hon Emily Coolidge finger the large diamond nestled against her rather bony chest and felt a familiar wave of boredom wash over him. This was his mother's country, the country in which he'd received much of his education, but he felt very little affinity with it. Or with the people who lived in it.

It felt empty. Soulless. Emily had to know he'd never choose her, or anyone like her, as the mother of his children. It made her behaviour inexplicable.

The brunette's finger moved again across the cool plains of the diamond droplet. There'd been a time, not so long ago, when that unspoken offer would have been appealing. In fact, he wouldn't have stopped to think about it. He'd merely have lost himself in mindless pleasure, content that Western women seemed to view these things differently.

'Will you be in London next week?'

Rashid twisted the champagne glass between thumb and forefinger, concentrating on the play of light on the liquid in his glass. He really hadn't thought much about who the mother of his children would be. It was always something for the future. Something far distant.

But now things were changing. He felt a mortality that had never touched him before. There had to be something inbuilt that made a man long to pass on his genes. To feel that he would go on...

Was that it? Was that what this gnawing dissatisfaction with his life was about? A wanting to set his place in history? To find meaning?

'I'm returning to town after this evening.' Again the brunette moved her hand suggestively across her low décolletage. 'Wouldn't it be fabulous if we could spend some time together before you fly back to Amrah?'

'No.' And then he cursed himself for what had been a staggering lack of good manners. His shoulders moved in an apologetic shrug. 'My father...'

Rashid let the sentence hang unfinished. The doctors, he knew, would do everything they could, but neither he, nor any man, could hope to foresee what the next few months would bring.

Emily leant forward and touched his hand, outwardly concerned.

Rashid studied her face. She didn't care. There was no genuine emotion in her painted eyes.

And he couldn't be bothered.

The truth of that slid into his brain like a dagger through silk. He wanted to shake these people off, move away, find space to breathe. And yet he had the responsibility of a guest towards his host's friends. A responsibility he was shirking.

It was a relief when a loud crack ripped across the general murmur of conversation. He looked out towards the formal gardens stretching down to the ornamental lake and at the white firework cascading down like some overblown pompom.

'Oh, my God, how lovely.' Emily unwound her overly

long body and stood, hand raised to shield her eyes as though that would somehow make it easier to see what was happening out in the landscaped gardens. 'Fireworks! Oh, Rashid, how beautiful.' She turned her long neck so she could look directly at him.

Another sharp crack, followed by a hiss and sizzle, and he caught sight of a particularly spectacular cascade of golden shards.

'I love fireworks!'

Vaguely, very vaguely, he was aware of the movement around the table. Chairs scraped back and then Nick's hand touching his arm. 'Coming to see?'

Rashid shook his head. He looked up and met his friend's understanding blue eyes. Nick knew why he was here and would be tolerant if his behaviour wasn't quite as it should be.

Rashid's head jerked upwards as he felt the spurt of anger flicker deep inside him. Under any other circumstances he wouldn't be here. Given half a choice he'd be back in Amrah, ready to spend precious time with his father if he was sent for. And he'd have been watching his brother's back, holding off the factions that were all too eager to turn recent events to their advantage.

His friend smiled and deftly manoeuvred the rest of the party outside. Rashid pulled a weary hand across his face and then let his eyes wander along the panelled walls. So different from home, but no less beautiful. Shelton Castle was a place of wealth. A little shabby, but in the English style of conserving all that was old regardless of fashion.

He'd come hoping to understand—and he didn't. The fifteenth Duke of Missenden was feckless and without honour. He fully deserved the destiny he had created for himself, Rashid thought, and if he'd scared him by coming here, so much the better.

Rashid was distracted by a flash of peacock-blue dipping in and out of the black-dinner-suited men clustered by the doors to the terrace. He sat back in his chair and watched Miss Pollyanna Anderson weave her way through the tightly packed throng watching the fireworks.

She was his one uncertainty. Where *did* she fit into all this? Last night he'd finally accepted Nick's statement that the dowager duchess and her daughter were not accepted by the late duke's children and therefore unlikely to be complicit in anything underhand.

But Pollyanna was too confident. She'd worked the room tonight with the assurance of someone who knew she belonged.

It had been Pollyanna who'd orchestrated the staff so they were largely inconspicuous. Pollyanna who'd managed the minor fracas earlier. He couldn't see her as someone passive. She appeared strong and capable.

So, given all that, was he prepared to accept Pollyanna Anderson's sudden desire to come to Amrah was a mere coincidence? His strong mouth twisted. And if it were not a coincidence, what he wanted to know was what she hoped to gain. And by what means did she intend to gain it?

His eyes narrowed. Did she hope to coerce him into silence by distorting what she saw in his country? Or was she some kind of a honey trap? Set to embarrass him and discredit his evidence?

That didn't feel right. She moved gracefully enough, but she didn't walk in a way that suggested she expected to be looked at. Her dress was a stunning colour, which brought out the deep blue of her eyes, but he doubted it had been made by any of the designers the women he'd spent time with would have deemed worthy of notice.

She *was* attractive, he conceded, but in a very English

way. Wide blue eyes, pale alabaster skin and hair the colour of desert sand. But no femme fatale. And, baring the fact he was certain she'd known exactly who he was and where he was to be found at any given time this evening, she'd not tried to approach him.

She'd been too busy working, controlling the events of the evening with a skill born of practice. He watched her as she paused, looking back towards the fireworks with a slight smile. Then she raised a hand to rub her neck and turned away. Her movements were rapid and she walked with obvious purpose across the highly polished floor towards a narrow door in the back wall.

It was the small furtive glance she made back across the now almost empty ballroom that had Rashid on his feet. Curiosity had always been his besetting sin and this was beyond temptation.

Rashid sidestepped the table and followed her across the ballroom. The door she'd walked through opened easily and he slid quietly into what appeared to be an intimate but ornately furnished sitting room. Gilt mirrors hung on the opposite wall and the furniture looked as if it belonged in a museum rather than a family home. All with a faded air of grandeur befitting one of England's foremost stately homes.

It took less than a second to locate Ms Anderson. She was sitting at right angles to the fireplace on one of a pair of brocade sofas, as yet completely unaware he'd come in. Via her reflection he watched her slip off her shoes and reach down to rub at her toes.

The rhythmic movement of her fingers over stock-inged feet was unexpectedly sensual and his eyes were riveted. Even more to the tantalising glimpse of her full breasts as the front of her dress gaped.

Rashid forced himself to look away and his eyes

snagged on the back of her neck, with the two soft tendrils of honey-gold hair that had escaped the tight twist she'd favoured. It was the kind of neck made to be kissed. Long. Soft.

Maybe he'd underestimated her success as a potential honey trap? Pollyanna possessed a natural sensuality.

'Ms Anderson, my name is Rashid Al Baha.'

Her head snapped round to look at him and her mouth formed an almost perfect 'o'. 'Wh—?'

'I apologise,' Rashid said, moving farther into the room, 'for disturbing you.'

She hurriedly returned her feet to the torturous-looking heels she'd been wearing and stood up, letting the soft folds of her dress mass around her ankles. 'No. That is, I…' One agitated hand twisted the loose curls back into her chignon. 'I'm sorry, did you need something?'

Rashid stopped a few feet away from her. 'I'm no great lover of fireworks.'

'Oh.'

Again that almost perfect oval. His eyes flicked across her flushed face and over a body that he knew Western convention would deem too curvaceous. She was not a conventional beauty, perhaps, but he felt a vague sense of disappointment that she was not a consolation prize.

Centuries ago he might have taken this woman in recompense for her stepbrother's sins. Maybe there'd been wisdom in that. It was just possible that a few weeks in the arms of Miss Pollyanna Anderson might go some way to dissipating his anger.

He watched the tremulous quiver of her full lips and felt a renewed rush of sexual awareness. Rashid clenched his teeth and forced himself to look at the famed Rembrandt hanging over the ornate fireplace.

'I thought this might be a good opportunity to talk,' he said, looking back at her, determined to regain control.

'Talk? I…' Her hand smoothed out the front of her dress, drawing attention to her curves.

'Or are you not aware your request to film in my country has been passed to me?'

'W-we did think it might have been.' And then she smiled.

She had an amazing smile. Rashid felt the full impact, particularly when it was combined with the feel of her hand in his. 'It's really kind of you, Your Highness.'

'Rashid, please.'

The beating pulse at the base of her neck was the only indication he had that she wasn't entirely comfortable. She had such pale skin. So white.

'Rashid,' she repeated obediently. 'And I'm Polly.'

It took him a moment to catch up. A moment he spent remembering that he needed to let go of her hand.

'Minty suggested I try to speak to you about it tonight, but I doubt I'd have had the courage.'

'Minty?'

'Araminta Woodville-Brown. She's the producer.' Polly hesitated. 'Hasn't she been in contact with you? I thought…'

Had she? Faced with a pair of clear blue eyes looking up at him he wasn't sure that he remembered.

'I thought that must be why you wanted to talk to me.'

'I've merely seen the paperwork,' he said in a voice that sounded overly formal. He couldn't seem to help it.

'Oh. Well…' she moistened her lips with the tip of her tongue '…Minty thinks…that is, she believes it would make a good programme and I…'

She broke off again and took a deep breath. Then she smiled. Her blue eyes glinting with sudden laughter. 'I'm making a real hash of this, aren't I? I'm so sorry.'

If she'd been hoping to deliver a polished presentation in support of the application sitting on his desk she certainly was, but at this precise moment he was more inclined to approve it than he would have believed possible.

She took another deep breath and Rashid found himself watching the rise and fall of her breasts. The fact they were now demurely covered made it more erotic than anything the Hon Emily Coolidge had managed in a dress practically slashed to her navel.

'Perhaps I could get you something to drink and we could start again?'

'I need nothing.'

'D-do you mind if I pour myself some water?'

'Not at all.'

Polly walked over to the mahogany bow sideboard and lifted a glass from the top of the water jug, chinking the two together. The noise was loud in the quiet of the room. Behind her, Rashid stood perfectly still. He was like some great big black spider. Motionless, and poised to strike.

Did spiders strike? Not that it really mattered. Rashid Al Baha looked as if *he* might strike. And, honestly, the reality of him was unnerving enough without adding the curse of her imagination. Tomorrow morning, the *minute* she opened her eyes, she was going to ring Minty and tell her the next time she had a good idea for smoothing out a bureaucratic hiccup she was to do it herself.

'I—I always keep some water in here in case I need it,' she said, trying to regulate her voice. Her hand shook slightly as she poured and a splodge landed partly on the tray and partly on the wood.

Everything slowed to half speed as the water spread out on the highly polished surface. 'Oh, God, please no!' she said, swiping at it with her hand. 'Oh, help!'

This was like a waking nightmare and it couldn't be happening to her. It couldn't. What was it about her karma that sent everything around her into free fall? Her fingers made no impact on the puddle of water and she turned round, looking for something that would be more effective.

'Here.' Rashid stepped forward, holding out a clean, starched white handkerchief.

She grabbed it and started to mop up the water, then carefully wiped the underside of the glass. 'Thanks. I'm not usually that clumsy.' And then, 'Actually, I am. I'm jinxed,' she said, handing back his handkerchief. 'But, look, no permanent damage. I live to destroy another day.'

She looked up and caught the waft of something tangy on his skin. A clean masculine smell. And she could see the dark shadow on his chin.

Powerful. That was the only word to describe Rashid Al Baha. It was apt for everything about him. Hard, masculine features, a honed physique that confirmed everything she'd read about his predilection for dangerous sports and a steady blue gaze that was startling against the black of his hair.

'Th-that sideboard came to Shelton in seventeen ninety-two.' Polly could feel the heat burning in her cheeks. 'It would be dreadful if I was the first person in all that time to put a mark on it.'

Rashid smiled. He'd smiled before, politely, but this was something different. For the first time it reached his eyes. Maybe he was human, after all? Wouldn't that be a surprise?

'I'm sorry. Please take a seat.' She pulled at the chain around her neck. 'I should have said that before. I'm afraid I'm a little nervous.'

That devastating smiled widened. 'There is no need to be.'

'You clearly don't know Minty. I'm no good at this type of thing.' Polly took her water with her and sat back down in the corner of the sofa. 'She'd do this so much better than I can.'

Rashid chose the sofa opposite. His eyes were still firmly resting on her face. It was unsettling. And that was putting it mildly.

'Take it to him.' Minty's final words to her were echoing in her head. She was fairly sure her friend hadn't factored in spilling water over a valuable antique, tripping over her words and generally not being able to think of anything anyway. Her mind was a complete blank.

And all the while those blue eyes watched her. Polly looked away and gently chewed at her bottom lip.

'I would be interested to know how you come to be involved?' he prompted, as though he knew she was never going to be able to get started alone.

He had an amazing voice, too. His accent wasn't so dissimilar to the ones she heard every day, but the way he put his words together, the stress he placed on the syllables was certainly different. Unmistakably foreign despite his English-public-school education.

'I suppose it's because it was my idea. In a way. Although I didn't expect it would happen.' She raised her eyes back up to his face. 'Minty's the film-maker. She wants to make an hour-and-a-half programme which could be broken up into three half-hour slots. Something like that.'

His feet moved and Polly found herself looking down at his highly polished Italian shoes. She was sure they were Italian. Expensive and very beautiful. Everything about him screamed an understated wealth. The kind of wealth that could buy a racehorse like Golden Mile as an individual rather than as part of a consortium. Even in her stepbrother's world that was unusual.

And here she was, sitting in the North Sitting Room with her heart in her mouth and her future, it would seem, resting on her ability to convince this man it was a good idea.

'With you presenting?'

'Yes, that's the idea.'

Rashid inclined his head. He was like a panther. The thought slid into her head. That was a far better analogy than a spider. He was all contained power, unpredictable and dangerous.

'I know we'd be the first film crew allowed into Amrah—'

'The second.'

'Second?'

'When my grandfather became King he was eager to open our country to the West. Fourteen years ago he allowed a programme to be made and the result was deeply offensive to both my family and our people.'

Talk about wanting the ground to open up beneath you. 'I didn't know that.'

Any other man and she'd have asked what had been offensive about it, but she didn't feel she could. There was an impenetrable barrier around Rashid Al Baha.

Polly moistened her lips and tried to find the words that would convince him that their intention was not to offend. Not in any way.

'Our programme would focus on Elizabeth Lewis's journey across Amrah in the late eighteen eighties. We'd like to retrace her steps, see some of the things she describes.'

'Such as?'

'The desert. Fortresses.' This was so difficult. She was

floundering and she knew it. She hadn't thought much about what she would see as the decision wasn't hers. 'Camel-riding. Maybe even camel-*racing*. I believe she did that at one point.'

Rashid sat back on the sofa. 'An important part of Amrah's culture, but not one that is generally looked on favourably in the West.'

'But the king has forbidden child jockeys by law. It— it was that,' she struggled on, 'which people found difficult to accept. Over here, I mean.'

Was she imagining a hint of a smile in those cold blue eyes? He really was the most unfathomable man. But, if his reputation with women had any basis in reality, he must be able to use that smile to good effect sometimes.

What would that feel like? If Rashid Al Baha looked at her with desire? With wanting? She felt a slightly hysterical bubble of laughter start in the pit of her stomach and spiral upwards. If His Highness Prince Rashid bin Khalid bin Abdullah Al Baha turned his notorious playboy charm on her she'd run in the opposite direction. He was an absolutely terrifying man.

'I see. It is helpful to have it explained.' The smile in his eyes became more definite.

Polly just hoped she'd wake up in a few minutes and realise this whole conversation had never happened.

Of course he didn't need her to tell him what the international community thought about child jockeys. He was a highly educated man. A leader of men. He'd probably even been instrumental in implementing the ban.

She could feel the heat rise in her face and a dry, nervous tickle irritate the back of her throat. Just wait 'til she got Minty on the phone tomorrow. If it turned out she had known about the 'offensive' programme made earlier Polly was going to personally shoot her.

'What I meant to say was that we wouldn't be saying anything…contentious. It's more a human-interest type of thing. A personal journey.'

'Personal?'

'Yes. Well, yes. That's the plan.'

'But not yours?'

She shrugged. 'Only in as much as Elizabeth Lewis is my great-great-grandmother.'

'Your great-great-grandmother?'

'On my father's side.'

A frown snapped across his forehead. 'That wasn't in the paperwork.'

'I suppose because it's not really relevant, is it?'

For a moment Rashid said nothing. 'Her legacy is still remembered in Amrah.'

Polly risked a smile. 'I still don't know very much about her, but I gather she was…ahead of her time.'

This time she was left in no doubt that his eyes were smiling, but his voice was still dry. 'An unusual woman.'

Did he consider that a good or a bad thing?

'That's it, really. Minty and I made a short programme on Shelton Castle about two years ago—'

'I've seen it.'

'You have?' she asked, her eyes nervously flicking up. 'Anyway, it was fun—and quite successful in ratings terms so Minty found it easy to get the funding for this one. And, well, th-that really is it…' She tailed off lamely. 'She's put it all together and I know she'll be more than happy to talk it over with you. I'm just there to provide a personal connection to the subject.'

And because Minty was quite determined her friend would find a life for herself away from Shelton. There was no need to mention that. It made her sound incredibly wet.

Besides, Minty might change her mind when she heard

how this conversation had gone. If Rashid had even the slightest inclination to open his country to a film crew again he'd want to be sure the resulting programme would be well executed and she hadn't done much to instil him with confidence.

Rashid stood up in one fluid movement. It was that panther thing again. He was all restrained power and energy, his mind finding an outlet in movement, and yet she would never describe him as agitated. In fact, you couldn't really imagine anything much throwing this man off his balance.

All of a sudden she didn't care one way or the other. She'd done her best and that was all anyone could do. If this didn't come off something would. Life was like that. It couldn't go on for ever without a bend in the road.

Polly finished off the last of her water and stood up, cradling the glass in two hands. 'W-what do you think? Can we come?'

His blue eyes flashed across at her. 'There would need to be conditions.'

'Of course. Not that I'd have anything to do with any of that. But Minty was wonderful when she made the programme on Shelton. Everyone involved was really considerate of the castle and there was nothing intrusive or unpleasant about the experience.'

Much to her annoyance Polly could hear a tremor in her voice. She wanted to sound confident and yet, somehow, in front of this man it wasn't possible.

'She's your friend.' He brushed her comment aside as though it wasn't worth nothing. It was the spur she needed.

'The programme on Shelton was one of five Minty made about different English stately homes. No one complained. She's a talented and very successful documentary film maker.' Polly raised her chin. 'So, what do you think?' she asked, forcing herself to meet his eyes. There was nothing to see. Not by so much as a flicker did he give away what he was thinking.

'Why now?'

She'd been braced for an outright rejection and his question surprised her. 'Now? You want to know why now?' she echoed, and then gathered herself together. 'Because of the weather. If we want to film in the desert—'

Rashid cut her off. 'I will think about it,' he said, turning away and striding across the room.

Polly stood, slightly stunned as the door shut behind him. She drew in a shaky breath. Heaven help her. That had been scary. But…he *had* left her with a little bit of hope— and, even ten minutes ago, that was more than she'd expected.

CHAPTER THREE

POLLY adjusted her long dark head-covering, trying to pull it farther over her blond hair. 'How do I stop this thing slipping off?'

Pete, standing closest to her, gave the front a gentle tug. 'Maybe a hair clip? I don't know. Do your best. It's not required of Westerners to cover their heads unless they're entering a holy place.'

Yes, she knew. But Minty's thirty-two-page ring-bound instruction booklet had also said a simple covering was sensible in the heat and generally considered respectful.

'Just relax about everything. So, where is this inter-preter guy? Ali something, isn't it?' he said with a look over his shoulder at the cameraman.

Ali Al-Sabt. She knew that, too. She'd gone through Minty's 'bible' and highlighted anything that might be important in fluorescent yellow. She practically knew it verbatim, but there was no point saying anything.

'He should be holding up a card. Easy enough to spot,' Baz said, scanning the crowded concourse.

'You'd have thought.'

Polly let the conversation wash over her. The five men Minty had assembled were all veteran travellers. They'd worked together before, knew each other well and clearly considered her dead weight in their team. It didn't matter. She was here. And it was absolutely incredible.

There were people everywhere. The guidebook had said that Amrahis regarded travel as an event and that whole families tended to see their loved ones off and meet those coming home. It was all a world away from her quiet and controlled departure from Heathrow, but she loved it. The noise, the bustle, the general excitement of the place.

'There! John's over there.'

A hand waved high above the crowd and Polly allowed Pete to steer her towards it, struggling to keep the wheels of her case straight.

A smiling man in a traditional white *dishdasha* nodded as they approached. *'As-salaam alaykum.'*

Polly murmured, *'Wa alaykum as-salaam.'* Which she seriously hoped meant 'Peace to you' or something like. Leastways that had been what her *Phrases for the Business Traveller to Amrah* had said, though her pronunciation was bound to be hit and miss despite the accompanying CD.

'This is Ali Al-Sabt—'

Behind them there was a loud shout and then a general hum of excitement. Polly's eyes went to the glass-protected VIP walkway, high above. At first she noticed the speed at which a group of men on it were walking, their sense of purpose—and then recognition hit her.

She felt as though her stomach had plummeted a couple of hundred feet. Even in the traditional robes of his country Rashid Al Baha was unmistakable. *Powerful.*

For the tiniest fraction of a second she fancied his footsteps slowed and his eyes met hers. She felt as though everything around her had frozen in a blur of colour.

There was only him…and her. Everyone else was as still as if they'd been paused by a TV remote. He looked directly at her. She was sure he did.

For a moment.

And then the world around her restarted, the noise of the concourse louder than before.

'That's Sheikh Rashid Al Baha. He must be returning from the summit in Balkrash.'

Polly wasn't sure which member of the team said that. She watched as Rashid disappeared from sight, still feeling a little shell shocked. She wasn't alone either. Judging from the reaction of the people around her, the Crown Prince's second son enjoyed a film-star status in his own country. There were fingers pointing all around. An excited chattering, which punctured the general hubbub of airport noise.

'What was the summit about?' she asked, bending to adjust the label on her bag.

'Perhaps best if we don't ask those kind of questions,' Steve, the one American of the team, said quietly. 'Let's keep ourselves out of the politics. Contravene that one and I guess we'll be on the first plane out of here.'

Polly agreed and stood quietly by while they waited for Graham to join them with all their equipment.

Seeing Rashid had brought back all the feelings she'd experienced when she'd met him at Shelton. He unsettled her. *Worried* her. It wasn't as though she felt he was attracted to her. Not that. It was that he…was watching her.

Watching her, looking for something that would mean he could make a decision about her. And because she knew he wasn't a man to have as your enemy it…*bothered* her. At least, she thought that was what she thought.

'Ready to go, Polly?' Baz said, coming behind her.

She nodded and let herself be steered towards the exit.

Once outside the intense heat hit her like a wall, driving everything else from her mind. She'd come expecting the temperatures to be high, but this was searing. Direct sunlight made her grateful for the scarf she had fashioned into a hijab covering her head. Less about modesty, perhaps, and everything about practicality.

'Please to come this way,' Ali said, indicating a line of waiting cars. Sleek, expensive and so black you might imagine they'd been dipped in oil. And more incredibly they were surrounded by uniformed guards. *Guards with guns.*

'Please. This way.'

Polly looked over her shoulder in time to see Pete duck down into the third car. Graham was anxiously watching their expensive equipment safely stowed away, and John, Baz and Steve had already vanished.

'Miss Anderson,' Ali said, indicating the second car. As she moved towards it the door was held open. Disorientated, she meekly did what was wanted, only hesitating when she realised there was a man already inside. A man she recognised.

'You?' she said foolishly.

Rashid Al Baha's blue eyes met hers. 'As you see.'

'I—I wasn't expecting to see… I mean…' *Oh, hell!* Polly pulled at the scarf covering her blond hair in what she recognised was a nervous gesture. 'Were you supposed to be meeting us? I'm sure we weren't told—'

His eyes seemed to dance. 'This is a spontaneous gesture of hospitality. There is no way I could have arranged my timetable today to coincide with yours.'

'Oh.' And then, rather belatedly, 'Thank you.'

'*Afwan.*'

You're welcome, she mentally translated, foolishly pleased the hours she'd spent poring over her phrase book were paying dividends. 'Are you sure we're allowed to be travelling together?'

Rashid settled himself more comfortably in his seat, resting his head back on the rest. 'You have an inaccurate view of my country.'

'I merely wondered whether it was appropriate with you being a member of the royal family.'

'Ah.' He turned his head so that he could look at her. 'I think you'll find that, as a member of the royal family, I'm permitted to do as I choose.'

Polly wasn't sure what to answer. Her explanation hadn't been true either, because she *had* wondered whether it was usual for a woman to travel alone in a private car with an Amrahi man who wasn't a family member. And it seemed Rashid was totally aware of that. His blue eyes were still glinting. Teasing.

Well, if he didn't care, why should she? This wasn't her country. She deliberately concentrated on fastening her seat belt. With the door shut and the tinted windows closed the atmosphere was pleasantly cool. Polly sighed and settled back into the softest leather seat she'd ever sat in. Soft as butter. She let her fingers rest on the suppleness of it and tried not to think how close Rashid Al Baha was to her. Or how much he unnerved her.

And he *really* did unnerve her. On every level there was. This close she could feel him breathe, strong and even. It seemed to pulse through her. As did her awareness of his taut body, thighs slightly apart and feet firmly planted against the sway of the car.

'You've just returned from a summit, I gather,' she said in an effort to break the silence.

'Yes.'

'D-did it go well?' Steve's words of caution came flooding into her mind. Politics was a no-go area. Part of the stipulations Rashid had made was that they didn't film anything that could be construed as military or politically sensitive. 'I don't mean to pry, obviously.'

He said nothing, merely watched her beneath hooded eyes.

'I still can't believe I'm really here.' Polly nervously pleated one end of her scarf. 'One minute I'm discussing whether we need to take the chandelier in the Great Hall down for cleaning and the next I'm here.'

Not the greatest conversational gambit she'd ever tried, but it was the best she could do. Every sense she had was throbbing with awareness. Every hair on her body standing to attention. She couldn't remember reacting to a man like this…ever. But then she'd never met a man quite like him.

Polly turned to look out of the tinted car window. Partly because she needed to have something other than Rashid Al Baha to focus on, and partly because she was captivated by what she was glimpsing.

The guidebooks she'd devoured hadn't really prepared her. She'd come expecting desert and wide blue skies and was confronted by modern glass, steel constructions and six-lane motorways.

'Amrah is a place of great contrasts,' Rashid said, as though he'd been able to read her thoughts.

'I had no idea Samaah would be like this. How old a city is it?'

He shifted in his seat, drawing her attention back to him as much by that as his voice. 'Centuries old, but its current incarnation is only forty. It has become a financial centre and brought a great deal of wealth to the country.'

She'd known that. Only that wasn't part of Elizabeth Lewis's story and she'd not focused her attention on what that would mean. 'Amrah doesn't have oil, does it?'

'Some, but the reserves are fast running out.'

Polly turned again to look out of the window. She watched as the buildings sped past, unwilling to miss anything.

If they'd arrived by sea, she knew from guidebooks she'd have been met with fortified ramparts dating back centuries. A testament to its troubled history. But this...was all so newly constructed.

'Are you disappointed?'

'Stunned.'

'We have the camels and the Bedouin tents, too.' His voice was laced with humour.

Polly turned her head to look at him and smiled. Her first since getting into the car. She settled back into her seat. 'Do you spend much time in the desert?'

'Like most of my countrymen I return at least once a year to reconnect myself with my heritage. A tradition, if you will. Something you English seem to understand.'

He said it as if she were a different species. 'You're half English.'

'My mother is English, but I am entirely Arab.'

How did he manage to turn his voice to flint? Polly adjusted her scarf, tucking one end carefully over her shoulder.

'I'm flattered you have so obviously researched me,' he continued, his voice slicing through the silence.

Polly glanced up at his calmly arrogant face. Did he honestly think that? That she'd consciously sat down and 'Googled' him?

She *had*. But she'd infinitely prefer it if he didn't think it. 'Merely read the magazines in the hairdresser's,' she corrected. 'You're often featured. Being royalty.'

'Then I should be the one asking the questions, perhaps.'

'There's nothing particularly interesting about me—' She broke off as she caught sight of the Majan International Hotel. 'Isn't that where we're staying?'

'There's been a change.'

Polly looked at him sharply. 'What kind of change?'

'I have decided to offer you the hospitality of my home while you are in Samaah. You and your colleagues,' he added as blandly as though he hadn't seen her quick glance through the back window to make sure they were still being followed.

She wasn't particularly reassured. Why was he doing this? He might have given them permission to film here, but even Minty hadn't imagined he'd wanted them here.

'Is that a spontaneous decision?'

'Not at all. How else could I have arranged for cars to be here to meet you?'

Quite. And Polly had the definite feeling very little in Rashid's life was left to chance.

'My sister is waiting to receive you. I was to have joined you later.'

His sister?

'Is it far from the airport?'

'No.'

Through the window to her left Polly could see they were still flanked by motorcycle outriders. It deflected her interest. 'Are they necessary?'

'It is wise.'

'Because we might be attacked?'

'Because I might be,' he returned coolly.

Rashid watched the blond Englishwoman process that. He could sense her uncertainty, see the questions she wanted to ask but felt she couldn't. For now that suited him perfectly well.

He stretched. 'It is a minimal threat but a significant

one, particularly while there is uncertainty about Amrah's political future.'

'I've read about that.' Her blue eyes met his. 'I was sorry to hear your father's ill again.'

Just that. No spurious sympathy in her face. He'd spent much of last week receiving condolences from men he knew would be pleased to hear his father had died and one of his more conservative uncles named as successor. Words meant nothing, but her quiet statement felt genuine.

It was that dichotomy again. The difference between what he knew and what he felt. She *seemed* genuine—but there was no one as plausible as someone who was making it her business to appear so.

'His doctors have been able to buy him a few months, but I think he will shortly be in paradise.'

'I'm so sorry.'

'I think your sympathy should be reserved for the people he is to leave behind.'

Pollyanna clutched at her scarf as it threatened to slide off her head. 'That's what I meant. It's incredibly hard to lose a parent.' Then, 'Are you sure this is the right time to have visitors like us? We would be perfectly comfortable at the hotel. And we only mean to stay in Samaah for a couple of nights.'

'I'm aware.'

'Wouldn't you rather be with your family?'

'If I'm needed I will be called.'

He watched her hesitate and then bite back whatever observation she had been tempted to make. That was just as well. He'd given more away in that single sentence than he'd intended.

Her perfume, light but exotic, swirled around him like a wisp of smoke. It seemed to drug his mind, pull truths from his lips he'd prefer left unsaid. And the truth was she was probably right. This wasn't the best time to have visitors in his home.

And certainly not this one.

Despite the dossier he'd read on Miss Pollyanna Anderson he remained uncertain of her motives in coming here. And, until he was, he'd every intention of controlling everything about her visit.

'Your family is well?'

Her blue eyes widened slightly. 'My mother's well enough.'

'And your brothers?'

'I don't have any brothers.'

It was very convincing. Yet she presumably chose to live in the home of her mother's stepson, a man he knew for a liar and a cheat, because she wanted to.

'I should have said stepbrothers,' he corrected smoothly. 'Your mother's late husband had three sons, I believe?'

'Yes. Anthony, the current Duke, is well, but I haven't seen Benedict or Simon for months. They rarely come to the castle.'

Did he believe that? All three brothers were directors of Beaufort Stud Farm with a financial stake in its success. It was inconceivable one brother should act alone in what was a family business.

Polly twisted her gold chain bracelet with long, slender fingers. *She was nervous.* He had to be wary of her, yet when he looked at her he found himself wanting to reach out and place a kiss on the inside of her wrist.

He wanted more than that if the tightening of his body was anything to go by.

Another time, another place. Rashid let the silence stretch between them. His brother had asked him to act as his right arm and Hanif couldn't afford negative publicity in the West. Not now. Not when his grandfather was looking to him to keep Amrah's financial markets steady and praying for an easy handover of power.

For now there was no choice but to keep this film crew close. Time enough to decide how much freedom he could allow them. Plenty of time to reach a conclusion about Pollyanna Anderson.

The cavalcade approached the outer gates of his home. He felt Pollyanna stiffen beside him and she turned to look at him with wide eyes.

'Welcome to my home,' he murmured.

'I-it's so beautiful.'

'Shukran.'

The gates opened seamlessly and the cavalcade moved forward, coming to a gentle stop. Polly unfastened her seat belt and adjusted her scarf once again, wrapping it tightly round her hair and letting both ends fall down her back. Even through the heavily tinted windows the magnificence of the place they'd been brought to was immediately obvious.

And it was old. How old she couldn't possibly judge, as the architectural style was completely unknown to her. Her door was opened and Polly accepted the wordless invitation to get out of the car. She stood, speechless, looking up at the white marble columns and the huge carved wooden doors, as intimidating as they'd surely been designed to be.

So incredibly beautiful. Breathtaking, really.

'Not bad, is it?' Pete remarked, coming up to stand beside her. 'I'm sorry you had to travel with Sheikh Rashid alone. You were there one minute and not the next. I'm not sure how that happened.'

Didn't he? Polly was in very little doubt. She watched

as Rashid paused to speak to one of his staff. She had no doubt he'd orchestrated everything that had happened. Nothing at all was left to chance.

Which meant he'd intended to ride with her alone. Intended to talk to her.

'Better be a bit careful about that. He's got a reputation. Probably because he's not allowed to play at home, if you know what I mean.'

Polly's eyes involuntarily wandered over to where Rashid was.

'But those rules might not extend to you since you're English. I can't believe this,' Pete said, looking about the palace with professional interest. 'It's incredible. I wonder if we can wangle filming here.'

Rashid walked towards them, an Amrahi prince to the ends of his fingers, Polly thought. And, for the first time in her hearing, he spoke in Arabic she didn't understand.

'Come. We will have refreshments.' The interpreter was almost beside himself with excitement. He was hovering about and practically rubbing his hands together in glee.

John moved closer to where she was standing and spoke quietly, 'This is a quite amazing honour. Try to follow my lead if you can. Hospitality is very important in this part of the world. There will probably be some kind of coffee-drinking ritual.'

Polly nodded and moved to follow. John stopped her. 'It's possible you might not be included. You might be taken to have refreshments with the women. I don't know. Just go with the flow. No point in upsetting him.'

She wasn't at all happy with that. The idea of being taken off, goodness only knew where, to make conversation with women who might or might not understand her language wasn't appealing. Particularly when she knew

Rashid was perfectly able to bend things to his will if he wanted to.

Still, she'd fight that battle if she had to. Polly adjusted her scarf once more, conscious of the heat burning through the dark fabric.

Rashid came to stand within six feet of her. 'I wish to introduce you to my sister, who is acting as my hostess and who will be able to help you with anything at all while you are staying in my home.'

'Thank you.' She looked past him to where a very beautiful woman was standing.

'My sister, Her Highness Princess Bahiyaa bint Khalid bint Abdullah Al Baha. Bahiyaa, this is Miss Pollyanna Anderson.'

The other woman moved forward to shake her hand. Polly automatically extended her own.

'You are very welcome, Miss Anderson.'

'Polly, please.'

'And I am Bahiyaa.'

Older than Rashid? Younger? She couldn't tell.

'You must be tired from your flight.'

Polly wasn't sure about that. The only thing she knew with certainty was that beside Bahiyaa she was impossibly creased. Minty's guide to all things Amrahi hadn't led her to expect anything like the exquisite gold embroidery on Bahiyaa's tunic, or the carefully co-ordinated scarf she wore over her head. The sunlight caught the gold bangles at her wrist and the overwhelming impression was one of shimmering beauty.

Erring on the side of caution, she, on the other hand, had picked a long-sleeved too-thick cotton top and paired it with an ankle-length linen skirt, both in olive-green. In the glamour stakes she was coming a very poor second.

'Shall we move in out of the heat?'

It seemed to be expected that the men would go first. Somehow with Bahiyaa beside her that didn't seem rude. It was simply different from the way things were done in England. And, anyway, she'd never quite understood why it was polite to encourage a woman into a room first. She always hated being thrust into a room of people she didn't know.

They walked across a central courtyard and through another pair of intricately carved wooden doors. The ceiling of the room beyond soared and Polly's eye was immediately captivated by the geometric decoration that seemed to cover every available surface.

Another pair of doors, another room beyond. And then they came to a room that was exquisitely beautiful for an entirely different reason. Glass doors had been opened out onto a garden. Polly couldn't see much of it but the scent of flowers wafting in was heady. *Roses.* Was that possible? Surely in these kinds of temperatures they must be incredibly difficult to grow?

A low table was central to the room and around it there were long couches in rich port-coloured silk. Polly watched carefully as Bahiyaa sank gracefully down and copied her, carefully tucking her skirt around her legs.

'As soon as you have had some refreshments I will take you to your room,' Bahiyaa said with a warm smile. 'By then your luggage will have been unpacked.'

Would it? Oh, heck! Polly had this terrible mental picture of the contents of her suitcase. She'd thought she'd imagined every possible scenario, but staying in an Amrahi palace hadn't been one of them. Having staff unpack for her was another.

Opposite, John was lounging comfortably on his couch, deep in conversation with his host. Minty had said she'd wanted him particularly because he'd worked so often in

Arab countries. He did make it look easy, but all the other team members seemed to be taking this whole experience in their stride. The Amrahi interpreter was smiling as though his life would never reach a greater height than this moment.

Polly tried to think of it in terms she would understand. This must be like being invited to Royal Lodge, the Duke of York's home. And, yet, it wasn't quite the same because the Al Baha family wielded real power rather than mere influence.

Today, only a few hours ago, Rashid had been at a summit with other Arab leaders. When she stopped to think about it, how *incredible* was that? She understood how important it was they kept themselves out of Amrahi politics, but how could you not be curious to know what had been discussed? A summit was something that would be reported worldwide. The decisions made there would impact on a whole region.

And *this* man was a part of that.

'Playboy sheikh' maybe, but on his home turf he was something else entirely. Every eye in the room seemed to be resting on him. It was his personality that was the dominant force.

'This is your first visit to Amrah?' Bahiyaa asked.

'My first visit anywhere, unless you count a long weekend in Paris with some university friends.'

'Then we must make absolutely sure your stay is delightful.' She paused while staff quietly came in with small plates of fresh dates, recognisable but only just. They were plump and almost jewel-like. Another couple brought plates of what looked like deep-fried balls together with bowls of a syrupy-looking sauce.

She'd read about the importance of coffee in this part of the world in her travel guides, but she'd expected her first experience of it would be in one of Samaah's modern coffee houses.

And she'd not expected to be tasting it under Rashid's watchful eye. He was aware of everything. A little out of her sight line, but she was certain he was listening to her conversation with his sister while he conducted a different one.

Polly had never felt so out of depth in her entire life. Not even when her mother had first announced her engagement to Richard and her bedroom had moved from the staff quarters to the family wing. That had been strange. But *this* was completely and utterly alien. There were no familiar points of reference at all.

She cast a surreptitious glance in his direction. Rashid's mother might have been English, the largest part of his education undertaken in her country, but it was hard to believe Rashid had had any Western influences in his life at all.

A man walked forward holding a silver tray on which was a type of coffee-pot and eight small china cups. He stopped by Rashid, who murmured something in Arabic before pouring coffee into one of the cups. Then he sipped. Placing the empty cup back on the tray, he poured a second cup and passed it to her.

She knew enough about this ritual to know it was considered the height of bad manners to refuse. Careful not to touch his fingers, she took hold of the handle-less cup with her right hand, as instructed in Minty's 'bible', and looked down into a thick translucent yellow drink.

It looked…foul, if she was perfectly honest, and it smelt incredibly strong. Polly looked at Bahiyaa for guidance as to whether she was expected to drink now or wait.

'This must be your first taste of *gahwa*. It is so much a

part of our culture that I often forget how strange it is to Western visitors. I think you'll find it quite similar to espresso.'

That wasn't especially comforting, since she'd never managed to acquire a taste for espresso.

'Try.'

Polly sipped. It was strong, with a mixture of flavours she found very strange. Her palate wasn't sufficiently developed for her to separate them out.

Bahiyaa reached out one heavily hennaed hand for a date and Polly copied her. The contrast between the bitter-tasting coffee and the sweet, succulent date was heavenly.

She looked up and caught Rashid watching her, his blue eyes openly focused on her. Her stomach clenched in recognition. Somehow, and she honestly didn't understand how, this man attracted her. Not just that. He *mesmerised* her.

Charisma. Power. *Danger.* He took her world and he changed it. He made her feel as though everything she'd ever known was now open to question. Every fundamental belief about how men and women reacted to each other now needed to be rethought.

Rashid's piercing blue eyes burned through her. The heavy scent of roses, the bitter taste of coffee in her mouth, the feel of heat surrounding her all combined. Polly watched, fixed like a rabbit in headlights, as Rashid drank his coffee.

She noticed the movement of his throat as he swallowed. Noticed the way his hand held the cup. Strong, beautiful hands. The kind of hands you would want to caress your body. And then her eyes travelled up to his lips. The kind of lips you would *want* to kiss you.

This was fantasy. She didn't know him. Knew very little about him, even. He wasn't, and couldn't ever be, part of her world, but what she was feeling was as old as time itself. She knew it, even though it frightened her.

She wanted him. And that wanting had nothing to do with liking or a desire to nurture. It owed nothing to shared values and goals. All the things she thought were important. This was about passion. Desire. An instinctive knowledge that sex with this man would be amazing.

Polly raised a hand up to her forehead. Blood was pulsing in her temples and she felt as if an iron band were tightening around her chest. She couldn't breathe in the heat. There was only an overwhelming need to lie down. To sleep. To…

'Polly.'

She heard Bahiyaa's voice as though it were some way away. And then there was nothing.

Rashid was on his feet.

'She's fainted.' Bahiyaa looked up, Polly's wrist held in her hand. 'It must have been the heat.'

He stood back as water was brought in a large iced jug and placed on the central table.

'Polly? Can you hear me?'

There was no sign of life other than the gentle rise and fall of her breasts. Her blond hair was splayed out across the ruby fabric of the couch. She looked pale and vulnerable. Beautiful. Rashid clenched his hands into fists by his side. His sister was certainly right in thinking that Polly had fainted, but he was less certain the cause was the heat.

Whatever it was that had passed between them was mutual. He'd seen the open desire in her eyes, read her thoughts as clearly as if she'd spoken them aloud. He'd seen the surprise in them, too, and knew she wasn't used to reacting to a man the way she did to him.

He watched her eyelids flutter and the soft parting of

her lips. 'Gentlemen, might I suggest I show you the rose garden while Ms Anderson recovers?' he said, his voice clipped. 'My sister will stay with her.'

The words were sensible, but Rashid stayed looking down at Polly.

'I will come and tell you how she is later,' his sister promised, brushing a gentle hand across Polly's forehead.

He wanted to push her aside. If there were no one in this room it would be his hand touching her face… And he *wanted* that with an intensity that amazed him.

'Rashid.'

Still he hesitated.

'Rashid,' Bahiyaa prompted again, 'you have guests.'

It had been no part of his plan to find Polly Anderson sexually desirable. And, yet, in that moment when he'd looked at her bravely drinking her first cup of *gahwa* he'd felt something shift.

He swore silently. No, before that. He'd felt it back in Shelton Castle. It was why Polly was in Amrah now when the sensible course of action would have been to refuse their application to film.

They were here because *she* fascinated him. Against all logic.

And his sister knew that. Her dark eyes looked up at him, a soft smile on her lips. She *knew*.

Rashid forced his hands to relax by his sides. It was the lure of the forbidden and he *would* master it. He had no place in his life for a woman like Pollyanna Anderson—even if she were not related by marriage to a man he fully intended to ruin.

'I'm sure my sister will manage better alone.' Abruptly he turned and moved towards the garden.

CHAPTER FOUR

POLLY awoke in a comfortable bed, cool cotton covering her, and it took a moment for her to realise where she was. Not at Shelton. Not any more. She was in *Rashid's* home. *Rashid Al Baha's palatial home.*

Her eyes took in the strange room. Presumably she'd been carried here because she sure as heck couldn't remember walking. *Carried.*

Polly raised a hand to shield her eyes, as though that would block out the image of that. Who had carried her? One of her colleagues? *Rashid?*

The last thing she actually remembered was the world slipping away and the overwhelming feeling of sickness that had accompanied it.

'There is nothing to worry about,' a female voice spoke softly. 'You fainted in the heat.'

Polly took her hand away and looked across the shadowy room to where Princess Bahiyaa was sitting reading by soft lamplight. Rashid's sister set the book down on the small hexagonal table and stood up.

'The heat and humidity here in Samaah is very different from anything in England. I should have arranged for refreshments to be served in an air-conditioned part of the palace,' she said, pouring out a glass of water from the jug set out beside the bed. 'I'm so sorry.'

Polly raised herself up on her elbow and pulled the pillow up behind her, only then noticing she was still in her clothes. Time to be grateful for small mercies. 'Carried' was humiliating enough, 'undressed' would have been terminally mortifying.

She brushed her hair off her face. 'I've never fainted before. I'm really embarrassed.'

'There is no need. The fault is mine.'

It wasn't. Polly knew it wasn't, but then it hadn't been her fault either. Nor had it been Rashid's, but his blue eyes were the last thing she remembered.

'*Shukran,*' she said, accepting the glass Bahiyaa gave her.

'Do you speak Arabic?'

'Only a few words and I'm not sure how useful they'll be.' She took a sip of water. '"*Ma-atakallam arabi*" might be, I suppose, but there's not a lot of point in saying "I don't know much Arabic" in anything other than English.'

Bahiyaa laughed. 'It is lovely that you have tried. May I?' she asked, indicating the side of the bed.

Polly nodded.

'While you were sleeping I arranged for some of my clothes to be brought for you. I saw that much of what you have will be uncomfortably warm even at this time of the year.'

Princess Bahiyaa had seen the contents of her suitcase. Oh...*hell*! Polly's toes squirmed at the thought of how she'd packed her case: socks balled down the sides and underwear she really should have binned months ago tucked inside her interpretation of 'modest and conservative' clothing. 'I couldn't, I—'

'It is no matter. Please.' Bahiyaa smiled. 'And it is my

pleasure. And maybe you would like a refreshing shower,' she said, pointing at a door in the far corner, 'before having a little to eat? You will feel much better, I think.'

Polly glanced down at her wristwatch. She made a quick mental calculation. Five o'clock UK time would mean it was a little past nine in Amrah. Too late to be asking her hosts to organise food…

But…the prospect of food was too tempting to put up a really convincing fight. And a shower would be wonderful.

'I will organise it now and be back shortly.'

Polly waited until Bahiyaa quietly shut the door before setting her glass down on the side table and gingerly pushing back the light covering that had been placed over her. The floor beneath her feet was tiled and cool. The room was impossibly beautiful, with dark wood furniture that was so burnished it seemed to shimmer.

Carved wooden screens were at the windows and bright jewel-coloured fabrics were draped over *the* most enormous bed. Polly bit back a smile. There'd be room for a sheikh and his entire harem in a bed that size. It was incredible and, if she set her English reserve to one side for a moment, wasn't it just the most exciting thing to stay in an Amrahi palace rather than some impersonal hotel?

Her great-great-grandmother would certainly have thought so. Elizabeth would probably have had no hesitation in borrowing Princess Bahiyaa's clothes either, Polly thought, fingering the silk of the pale pink tunic laid out across the foot of the bed. For just this little while wouldn't it be wonderful to set aside all of her inhibitions? To live boldly?

Polly let the tunic drop back on the bed and padded over to where Bahiyaa had said she'd find a shower. She stopped on the threshold, stunned by the acres of black marble and a highly decadent sunken bath.

Aware Rashid's sister could return at any moment, Polly opted for a shower, and in the quickest time possible, before scurrying back to the bedroom. Bahiyaa's clothes were waiting for her. Tempting her. The silver threads in the fabric glinting in the lamplight. She felt as if she'd got the devil himself sitting on her shoulder whispering, 'Just do it.'

Polly picked up the silk…trousers and stepped into them. She supposed that was what they were called. They were loose fitting with a drawstring waist and came in tight around the ankles. And were incredibly comfortable. Already she could feel that the fierce heat of Amrah's sun would be more bearable without a tight waistband.

And the tunic felt like gossamer. She'd never worn a fabric so light, or decorated with such exquisite embroidery. Minty's instruction to dress 'conservatively' and 'modestly' had suddenly taken on a whole new meaning. This outfit was far sexier than anything she'd worn before.

It was the colours, the geometric patterns in the embroidery and the way the silk caressed her skin. It was…*glamour* with a capital 'G'.

Taking the path of least conflict at Shelton meant she had precious little experience of that. The knack of survival had been to blend into the background as much as possible and no one wearing something like this could ever hope to do that.

She felt beautiful in it. She felt as if she really had wandered into an Arabian adventure. She felt like someone else and that was exciting.

There was a soft tap at the door.

'May I come in?' Bahiyaa called.

'Yes.' Polly moved to open the door. 'Yes, of course.'

'That pink is a wonderful colour for you,' Bahiyaa said, coming into the room. 'I thought it would be. It makes your pale skin bloom.'

If any woman had said that to her in England Polly would have found it strange, but coming from Bahiyaa it was charming. She smiled. 'You're very kind to lend—'

'It is a gift,' the other woman stopped her. 'Please.' She turned and picked up a loose wraplike cloak in the same shade of dusky pink. 'There is a little more before you are ready. This we call a *thub* and you wear it over the *dishdasha*.'

'The tunic's called a *dishdasha*? I thought that was for men?'

'Similar, but a little more fitted,' Bahiyaa said with a laugh. 'Women here are not so very different from those in your country. And men are the same the world over. These,' Bahiyaa said, pointing at the loose-fitting trousers, 'we call *sirwal*.'

'*Sirwal*,' Polly repeated obediently.

'And finally,' Bahiyaa continued, reaching behind her for a long length of fine pink silk, slightly darker than either the *sirwal* or the *dishdasha* but picking out some of the embroidery in the over jacket, 'you have a *lihaf*.'

'*Lihaf* not *hijab*?'

Bahiyaa smiled and gently arranged the *lihaf* in place. 'Arabia is made up of many countries and there are many tribes within each of those. Each tribe has its own traditions, its own way of dressing and distinctive dialect.'

'I didn't mean—'

'You are looking beautiful. All we need now is sandals. I thought that since we are a similar size you might be able to manage with a pair of mine? I am a European size thirty-nine.'

Polly was beginning to feel so overwhelmed by the whole situation she'd have put on anything—and it was magical to be given the chance to wear something so romantic and feminine. She slipped her feet into

Bahiyaa's high gold sandals, a size too big but perfectly manageable.

'Perfect.' Bahiyaa stepped back to admire the effect. 'Now come.'

Polly found it hard to pull herself away from the mirror. She looked completely different. Transformed. Bahiyaa laughed as though she knew exactly what Polly was thinking. 'I never understand why some Amrahi women adopt Western dress. Our traditional clothes are...deceptively seductive, don't you think?'

Sexy, Polly amended silently. Layers of finest silk that skimmed the body were *very* sexy.

'They're gorgeous.'

'Come. I thought you would enjoy eating in the cool of the gardens.'

Reluctantly Polly let Bahiyaa lead her away from the mirror. She'd never been one for admiring herself, but she couldn't quite believe she could look so different. Even more amazingly she *felt* different.

Bahiyaa led her through a maze of narrow corridors. Polly's eyes snagged on the intricately carved archways and a fleeting glimpse of a small courtyard filled with lemon trees in pots. Then they were back in the room in which she'd fainted.

'The rose garden is one of my favourite places,' she said, leading her outside. 'Rashid's, too.'

Polly could understand why. If anything the scent of roses was stronger now than in the heat of the day. And there were other unfamiliar smells. Jasmine, maybe?

'It is a romantic place, I think.'

Like something out of an old Hollywood version of *Arabian Nights*, a real mix of East and West. Polly followed, acutely conscious of how the heels of her borrowed sandals tapped on the mosaic-tiled floor and charmed by the creamy candles placed in large ornate holders.

Bahiyaa walked on in a jangle of gold bangles. 'These gardens were here in the time of your great-great-grand-mother.'

Were they? Really? Polly looked around with new eyes. Was she looking at something Elizabeth would have seen?

'You must ask Rashid to tell you something of their history.'

'Yes, I…' *will.* That was what she'd meant to have said, but the single word dried in her throat as Rashid came out of the shadows to meet them.

Unlike her, he was no longer in traditional Amrahi clothes. He wore jeans and a light cotton shirt open at the neck, his dark hair uncovered…

'He is something of an authority.'

Sexier even than she'd thought him at Shelton. More intimidating than he'd ever been before.

'Bahiyaa.' He spoke his sister's name on a breath.

Polly glanced back over her shoulder as the suspicion Bahiyaa had orchestrated this 'accidental' meeting took hold and that her brother was not happy about it.

'I have brought your guest to see you, Rashid, now Polly is feeling so much better. Please,' his sister in-structed, gesturing towards a sumptuous pile of cushions on a raised dais, 'sit with Rashid for a while. He will love to tell you about these gardens while I organise for your food to be brought out here.'

Then, with a mischievous smile at her brother, she was gone.

Rashid's eyelids quickly came down to cover his ex-pression, but Polly was sure he didn't want her here. She was intruding. What was more she felt a little as though she'd been caught dressing up.

When she was in her own clothes, in her own country, Rashid made her feel uncomfortable enough. Here it was almost unbearable. And, face to face with Rashid again, it didn't take any thought to understand why she'd fainted. Around him she found it difficult to remember to breathe. He was scarily beautiful in an aggressive, masculine way.

And not at all likely to be interested in her. Best she remember that. A man who lived a life completely different from hers. With a very different moral code.

'Would you prefer to be alone? I—'

'No,' Rashid stopped her. 'I'm glad of your company.' He, too, indicated the richly coloured cushions. 'Please join me.'

Polly didn't believe him, but she sank down as gracefully as she could manage and carefully tucked her feet beneath her. Soles pointing away from him, as instructed in Minty's manual.

Polly looked up to find Rashid's eyes were glinting down at her. He was *laughing*. Heat washed over her face and with it a sudden, unexpected flash of anger. Polly tilted her chin. 'Am I doing this wrong?'

'No.'

'Then why are you laughing at me?'

The smile in Rashid's eyes intensified. 'You are charming. I wish all visitors to Amrah were as courteous and considerate of our customs.'

'I-I'm trying to follow the rules. There's no point coming here if you aren't...' her voice trailed off as he sat down beside her, close enough that she could feel the warmth of his body '...aren't going to make the effort.'

'I agree. I try to follow them myself.'

'You do?'

'I drink alcohol, but not when I'm in Amrah because it offends so many. Moving between cultures requires dexterity.' Rashid smiled.

His eyes moved over the fine fabric of her *dishdasha*, setting her on fire. He made her feel…out of control. As though she were entirely made up of hormones. 'B-Bahiyaa said I'd be more comfortable in something of hers.'

'And are you?'

'Yes.'

If it weren't for the way he was looking at her. At Shelton she prided herself on being able to handle any situation, but here…she couldn't. But it wasn't being in Amrah that made the difference. It was the garden. The night. *Rashid.* Mostly Rashid.

His clever face concealed so much more than it showed, but when his eyes danced they seduced her. They melted her from the inside out. And every now and then she fancied they hovered on her lips as though he might be thinking what it would be like to kiss her.

Her breath seemed to dry in her throat at the thought of what it would be like to have him kiss her. In her entire twenty-seven years she'd never felt her body wouldn't respond to the instructions of her brain before. She wasn't sure she liked him, but he was the most compelling man she'd ever met.

'You look very beautiful.'

Polly's eyes flew up to meet his. It would be so easy to believe he meant that. Seduced by the moment into doing goodness knew what.

If she wasn't sensible. If she didn't remember Rashid was known in the West as Amrah's playboy sheikh for a reason. Presumably women often dissolved in a pool of oestrogen at his feet. It would be much better for her self-esteem if she didn't become another conquest.

'I am glad you have recovered,' he said softly.

'So am I.' Polly's hands pleated the end of her *lihaf*, watching the silver threads glint in the candlelight.

'The heat can be punishing.'

Polly moistened her upper lip with the tip of her tongue. 'I—I bet the guys are dreading going with me into the desert. They must think I'm a complete liability now.'

'I doubt that.'

Polly dragged her eyes away from his. She'd had six years of making 'small talk'. She could do this. If she just kept breathing in and out he need never know she felt as though a million tiny ants had been let loose inside her. 'Are they joining us here?'

'Baz and John intended to swim here at the palace before having an early night. Graham, Pete and Steve have gone into Samaah. I suspect in search of alcohol in one of the international hotels. Do you wish you could have gone with your friends?'

Polly gave a sudden nervous laugh. 'If I said "yes" that would be a little rude, wouldn't it? And the guys aren't "friends". I met them for the first time at the airport.'

'Colleagues,' he amended.

'Even that sounds a bit grand. I keep pinching myself to prove I'm really here and not dreaming.' Polly turned her head at the sound of people approaching. Men. All dressed in simple white *dishdashas*. She watched wide-eyed as her food was set over a small burner to keep warm. The saffron-coloured rice dish smelt absolutely fantastic.

'This is *maqbous*,' Rashid said as one of the men spooned a portion into a shallow bowl. 'It's a popular Amrahi dish, although not confined to this region. You'll find the same in Oman and Saudi Arabia. Balkrash, too.'

Instead of handing it to her, the man placed it down on the low table in front of her and it was Rashid who passed it across. Then he spoke to the men in Arabic and they silently moved away, leaving behind tall glasses of layered fruit juice and a jug of iced water.

'I hope you will enjoy this more than *gahwa*.'

Polly looked back up into his teasing blue eyes. When he looked at her like that it was really very difficult to remember all the reasons why she shouldn't let herself relax into the moment. She'd had years and years of being responsible. It would be wonderful to act without thinking. To succumb to the playboy prince of Amrah, perhaps?

Crazy.

She carefully combined some of the white meat with the rice for a perfect first mouthful, glad she had something to do.

'It's spicy,' she said, surprised. 'And it's lovely. Are you not eating anything?'

'No.'

Polly felt a sudden wave of renewed embarrassment as she realised all this food was for her. 'You know, I could have waited until tomorrow. There was no need for Bahiyaa to—'

'It is our pleasure.'

It was really too late to protest too much. The food was there, she was hungry and it *was* delicious. She'd been too excited during her flight to eat much, not particularly inspired by what had been served either. 'Thank you.'

Rashid poured her a glass of iced water. He set that on the low table in front of her and, once she'd finished eating, she exchanged her empty bowl for the water. Ice, *ice* cold.

'I think I'm in heaven.'

'I always think that when I come home to Amrah.'

He smiled and Polly felt her own falter. 'Then why spend so much time away?'

He shrugged with typical Arab insouciance. 'I have business which takes me abroad. Hobbies.'

Oh, yes, she knew plenty about those. She'd seen the

smiling pictures of Sheikh Rashid Al Baha with assorted society beauties. It might help control her awareness of him if she remembered that.

'Like your stepbrother I am passionate about horses, but that is more of a mission than a hobby.'

Nothing like Anthony, then. The Beaufort Stud was a means to an end. Not a passion, certainly not a mission. Even Shelton wasn't. He saw the castle as a financial drain.

Polly took another spicy mouthful, determined not to dwell on how precarious Shelton's future was. She couldn't alter Anthony's personality, couldn't inspire him with her love for the castle, any more than his father had been able to. 'In what way a mission?'

'I want to see Arabia acknowledged as the home of racing.' Rashid placed his glass down on the table and looked at her. 'Every thoroughbred can trace its lineage back to one of three sires.'

'Yes, I know. The Darley Arabian, the Godolphin Barb and…the Byerly Turk,' she produced triumphantly, ridiculously glad her marshmallow brain had come up with something sensible.

Rashid sat back against the cushions. 'Trace their heritage back a little further and you discover all three have their roots in Arabia. Racing belongs here. What I have begun here is a fraction of what the Maktoum family have achieved for Dubai, but it will come.'

'Gambling is forbidden here, isn't it?' Polly said, after a moment.

'As it is in Dubai.'

Polly nodded. 'So that must mean your interest is tourism. Particularly since you said your oil reserves are running out. So, why,' she continued, slightly intimidated by the sudden narrowing of his eyes, 'why aren't you more enthusiastic about this documentary?'

'What makes you think I'm not?'

'Are you?'

His sensual mouth twisted into something approaching a smile. 'I have given my permission.'

Which was no answer at all. And he was watching her again as though he expected her to be trouble. She didn't understand why. 'Surely you want people to catch a glimpse of Amrah and be inspired to come here?'

He said nothing. Hard, flinty eyes looked at her, a muscle flexing in his cheek, then he leant forward to pick up his glass again and took a sip. 'Let us say I find it difficult to trust,' he said, at last.

'We really don't intend any kind of political comment. This documentary is to be entirely about Elizabeth Lewis.' Polly looked about the garden, foolishly hurt. There was no reason on earth why he should trust her. He didn't know her. It wasn't personal… 'Was this really here in the time of my great-great-grandmother?'

'It was created for her.'

'It was?'

'It's why there are so many roses. Tradition has it that Elizabeth missed the roses of her English home and so my great-great-grandfather conceived and planted this garden for her. You know they lived here for a time?'

Polly shook her head.

'After their adventure in the Atiq Desert in eighteen eighty-nine they stayed here for a handful of months.' Rashid settled back against the cushions once more, the fierce glitter in his eyes gone. 'You knew they became lovers within days of meeting?'

Polly nodded. The knowledge that their ancestors had been lovers made her feel shy. 'Dr Wriggley said they settled in Al-Jalini.'

'*Elizabeth* was settled there. When it became clear she

wasn't going to return home. It's a beautiful sea port and she lived there until she died in nineteen oh-four.'

'Alone?'

'No.' Rashid picked up one of the fruit juices and handed it across to Polly. 'Al-Jalini is the perfect place to live out a romantic idyll. I think King Mahmoud spent every moment he could with her, much to the anger of his wives. Theirs was an enduring love story.'

'But selfish.' She'd thought a lot about this. 'He was already married and so was she. And Elizabeth was a mother. I've read some letters which say her son was told she'd died and we know her husband drank himself to a pre-mature death. The scandal was too much for him, I suppose.'

'The son being your great-grandfather?'

Polly nodded. Those letters had made her cry. 'It's a strange feeling to be connected to someone as…colour-ful as her,' Polly said, searching for the right word, 'but when you start to think about the hurt she caused I can't like her particularly.'

Rashid picked up the second fruit juice and sipped, his eyes not leaving her face.

'I do like her courage and zest for living,' Polly said, stumbling on. 'I'd like to have that.' She'd really like to have that, but real life had intervened. She had respon-sibilities, people she cared for and who cared about her. *As Elizabeth Lewis had had.* 'I know I'd have stayed in England and tended my rose garden there. Not very exciting of me, is it?'

'It depends on the motivation behind the decision.'

'I couldn't have left my child.'

'Mothers do.'

His mother *had*, if what she'd read about him was true. If only there were a nice deep hole in which she could hide herself. For someone who prided herself on her social skills, she was doing appallingly.

She struggled on, 'And, maybe it wasn't as straightforward as it seems. These things often aren't.' She stopped her fingers pleating her *lihaf*.

'What became of the son?'

Polly forced a smile and said brightly, 'Oh, he married and had five children spread over two wives. The youngest son being my grandfather, who became a not particularly distinguished soldier with something of a drink problem. So perhaps *his* grandfather's early demise wasn't entirely due to Elizabeth. It would be nice to think that. My mother remembers her father as being very...handsome but ineffectual.'

'You didn't know him?'

'Oh, no, he died in his forties and his widow became a housekeeper and, family gossip has it, a little bit more to a Major Bradley.' Polly picked up her fruit juice and traced a finger across the condensation on the glass. 'Now, I do remember him. Not that I knew anything about the "little bit more". As far as I was aware she really did just look after his house. They never married.'

'And your mother?'

'Became a shorthand typist and eventually married my father. Who was a chef at Shelton.'

Rashid hadn't moved. His eyes were still on her face, his expression one of polite interest. She'd probably bored him rigid.

'What's in this?' Polly asked, holding out her fruit juice. 'I don't think I've tasted anything like it.'

Rashid moved one long finger up the glass. 'Avocado, orange, pomegranate and mango.'

She took another sip. 'I can taste the orange, but I'd never have guessed avocado. It's lovely.'

'I am glad you like it. Have you lived at Shelton Castle all your life?'

'On and off,' she said evasively. Rashid was being polite and she didn't want that. She wished, for perhaps the millionth time in her adult life, she were more like Minty. It would have been nice to have felt confidently sexy and flirted a little bit with a man who most certainly knew how the game was played.

But she was seriously out of practice. Like the clothes, the easiest way to maintain the peace at Shelton was to keep a low profile. Her life would have been immeasurably worse if Anthony had thought she intended to snare a society husband for herself. Far better to blend into the background.

'Go on,' Rashid prompted, his entire attention focused on her.

'Initially we had a house on the estate. Then he died and we moved out into the village. For a while.'

'But not for long?'

'No.' Polly made a great show of sipping her fruit juice as the silence stretched out between them.

'Please. If it is not intrusive I would like to know about your life.'

He really did sound as if he meant it. Goodness, but he was good. How incredibly easy it would be to allow herself to believe he really wanted to know all about her. *And how foolish.* She ought to have slipped some of those glossy articles in her handbag so she could remind herself how Rashid had become quite so adept at making a woman feel special.

Only she hadn't thought she'd meet him again. Certainly hadn't thought she'd be staying in his home. And couldn't have imagined he would turn any part of his attention on her.

'My mum continued to work at the castle and eventually she became the housekeeper. So we moved back. We had a suite of rooms in the staff quarters...until Mum married Richard,' she said, truncating years into the fewest number of sentences possible.

'Were you pleased?'

'Yes, of course.' She took another sip of her drink, adding when he said nothing, 'I suppose I was shocked, but they were very happy together.'

'And was that why you decided to come back to Shelton Castle after you finished university?'

How the heck did he know that? Surely Minty hadn't thought it necessary to provide him with a full CV...

He must have seen something of her surprise in her face because he smiled. A slight deepening of the tiny lines fanning out from his sexy eyes, which had her stomach perform a complete somersault. 'You have a first from Warwick University in English and Political Science.' Rashid adjusted his powerful body against the cushions, but only so he could see her face more clearly. 'That information was in the paperwork sent to me.'

Ah. If he knew about her interest in politics, maybe that went some way to explaining his concern at her involvement. He needn't have worried. Since leaving university the only politics she'd had time for were the internal ones going on at Shelton.

'My mother found it...difficult to adjust to being the Duchess of Missenden.'

'Difficult?'

'Difficult is probably not the right word,' she concurred. The truth was her mother had found it completely impossible. Anthony had been incandescently angry. Benedict and Simon very little better. 'Dukes don't generally marry their housekeepers. Not in England, anyway. So I came for moral support with Richard's blessing. I meant to spend just a year there but…' Polly shrugged '…time passed and I stayed. And then there was the accident and I…stayed again.'

Nothing like the art of British understatement. Six years of emotional turmoil neatly contained in a handful of sentences.

'Until now.'

'Until now,' she echoed with a smile. 'I think this is the first thing I've ever done entirely for myself. I hope I don't make a mess of it.'

'Why should you?'

'Well…' Polly pretended to hesitate '…there's having to speak directly at a camera as though it were a friend, coping with the heat…'

Rashid laughed and her chest grew tight, as though she'd swallowed too much air. 'How about you? I—I seem to have given you my life story from four years onwards.'

'I was under the impression you had researched me fairly thoroughly,' he said lazily, his voice little more than a rumble.

Her eyes flew up to meet his teasing ones and she felt as pinned as a butterfly in a collector's box. There was no getting away from sexy blue eyes that ripped through every preconception she'd ever had about herself.

'What do you wish to know about me?'

Where to start? It was difficult not to be fascinated by a man who was so completely different from anyone she'd ever met before. He was simply more. More arrogant. More sexy. More inscrutable. More charismatic. *More.*

And yet he had roots in her own country. Those compelling blue eyes reminded her of it. 'Do you really not feel remotely English? Not on any level?'

Rashid leant forward and tore off a piece of *rukhal*

bread and offered it to her. Polly took it and he tore off a second piece for himself. 'I think I made a choice.'

'Between being Arab and English?' She broke off the tiniest piece of her bread and put it in her mouth, watching the frown that formed on his forehead.

'You will have read something of my parents' divorce?'

It was scarcely a question but Polly nodded. She'd certainly done that. It was practically the first thing anyone wrote about him.

'I was eight at the time and very angry when my mother left. I wanted nothing to do with her. I identified completely with my father. My one aim and purpose was to be like him. And that meant embracing everything that was important to him. I wanted to expunge everything English from my life because he hated it.'

'So how did being given an English education fit into that?' she couldn't resist asking.

Rashid smiled. 'I went to the same boarding school and university as my father. Followed that up with a Sandhurst military training, as had my brother Hanif before me. And during the holidays I absorbed everything Amrahi. Poetry. Art. Music.'

'To please your father?'

'Initially. Even horse racing was his passion before it was mine. My father,' Rashid said, reaching for the water jug and refilling Polly's glass, 'insisted we were connected with our Bedouin heritage and the Bedouin have a long tradition as master horsemen.'

So, naturally, Rashid had wanted to excel. Polly accepted her glass back. 'I've only been to the races once in my life. The summer after Mum married Richard. To be honest it seemed more about gambling than sport. I suppose you *could* argue gambling is a sport.'

'Not in Amrah.'

No, not in Amrah. Polly took another piece of *rukhal* bread. 'So, if there's no revenue from gambling, how is the Samaah Golden Cup funded?'

'Private investment.'

'Yours?'

His dark eyebrows rose, the blue eyes beneath them glinting in amusement.

Polly bit her lip and shook her head slightly. 'That must be millions of dollars of "private investment".'

'Twenty-eight million.'

'That's crazy!'

'We have to look to the future. Tourism and international finance is vital to our economy.'

'And do you get a good return on twenty-eight million dollars?' she asked politely.

'I think so. I make sure that I do.'

Six words, but they sent a shiver down her spine. It reminded her of how he'd been at Shelton. That feeling that he would break whatever needed to be broken.

Rashid leant forward and tilted her chin up so he could look directly into her eyes. 'I have a habit of winning.'

'So I've read.'

Then his hand lightly stroked the side of her cheek, burning a trail across her skin. His eyes lingered on her lips. If he kissed her now she wouldn't be able to stop him—even though she knew this was all a game to him.

Humiliatingly, he must know she'd fall into his bed like a ripe greengage from a tree. Almost. There was still the finest steel of self-preservation holding her back.

Rashid's blue eyes glittered down at her, his thumb moving to stroke across her sensitive lips. Slowly. Very slowly, he moved to kiss her.

Her hands came up to hold him off, but one touch of

his lips had them snaking round his neck, pulling him closer. Beneath her fingers she felt the soft curling hair that touched the nape of his neck. Her mouth softened and she heard the guttural sound of satisfaction deep in his throat.

Winning. This was all about winning.

'No.' She pulled back, her breath coming in short sharp bursts.

Rashid's hands still cradled her face, his eyes locked with hers. 'Polly.' His deep voice breathed her name, sending renewed shivers coursing through her body.

'This isn't right. Please.'

His smiled twisted. Then he sat back, watching her face. 'I will escort you back to your room.'

'Th-thank you.' Polly felt by her side for her *lihaf*, which had fallen off unheeded. She balled it up in her hand as sudden cold whipped through her. He must think she was a complete idiot. Any other woman would have just closed their eyes and thanked their lucky stars.

Other women did.

'Come.'

She looked up to find Rashid was already standing. He held out a hand. Polly allowed him to help her to her feet. A faint breeze caught at the light fabric of her *dishdasha*, brushing it against the denim of his jeans.

Polly drew in a ragged breath. She just wasn't made that way. But she was under no illusions. If Rashid truly intended to 'win' she'd be powerless to stop him.

CHAPTER FIVE

RASHID stood looking out across the courtyard, the fountain anything but soothing. There'd been some semblance of normality as he'd escorted Polly back to her room. Years of experience had meant that he was perfectly able to talk about her proposed documentary, the arrangements that had been made to take them into the Atiq Desert, all the while pretending his body wasn't on fire for her.

He screwed up the piece of paper in his hand and aimed it towards the waste bin by the desk. It brushed the edge and fell neatly inside. Rashid looked away, back out towards the central fountain and jagged a hand through his hair.

He'd kissed her. It didn't matter he'd intended it as a kind of test. Somewhere between the thought and the action his motivation had changed. And he'd felt her tremble. Her lips had been warm and pliant against his. Her fingers had been in his hair pulling him closer, urging him on until the moment she'd stopped. Stopped *him*. The control had been all hers.

Rashid swore softly. Inviting them, *her*, to stay in his home had seemed such an inspired idea. He pulled an agitated hand across his face. It felt less inspired now.

'Rashid?'

He spun round to face his sister. She quietly shut the door and walked to stand next to him.

'Are you angry with me?' she asked in Arabic, her voice low.

'Do not bring her to me again. I will make my decisions in my own time and in my own way.'

Bahiyaa turned so she could look at his profile. 'I do not believe Polly is involved in anything criminal.'

'And you know that how?'

'I know my own sex, Rashid. I genuinely believe she is here solely to make this documentary. And,' she continued after a moment of silence, 'she is charmingly excited to be here. I don't think she has been used to have her wishes considered. Rashid, are you listening to me?'

He was listening, to every word. In his heart of hearts he didn't believe Polly was complicit in any crime either. Perhaps it was his sense of self-preservation that had made him cling to that idea longer than was reasonable?

Even so…it was still possible. The timing of their visit was damnable and the stakes were high. If anything appeared in the British press that Hanif's enemies could use against him, Rashid would never be able to live with himself.

Rashid straightened his spine, the expression on his face set as he looked down at his sister. 'Golden Mile *is* sitting in our stables unable to sire anything—'

'I understand that.'

'*Knowingly* sold as a stud horse by Polly's stepbrother.'

'But—'

He pulled an agitated hand through his hair once more. 'The ramifications of that will be far-reaching. There will be people, apparently *good* people, who have been persuaded to take pay-outs. People we know, Bahiyaa.'

'But not Polly. I do not believe it.'

He'd thought…it would be easy to *know*. By changing her plans, having her stay in his home with the opportunity to talk to her…

He hadn't expected desire to cloud his thinking.

He'd been prepared for everything but Polly with her wide eyes and soft curves. She seemed to be a woman of contradictions. At Shelton she had appeared so confident. The way she held herself, the way she moved, talked to people, managed difficult egos with quiet skill had suggested inner confidence. Here in Amrah she was eager to please, *anxious*…

Anxious because she suspected she was out of her depth and knew it?

Rashid left Bahiyaa at the French doors and sat down at his desk, picking up his fountain pen and twisting it between thumb and forefinger.

'What are you going to do?'

Without turning his head he knew Bahiyaa had moved to stand behind him. 'Here Polly can be closely supervised. While filming she can be equally monitored.'

'About Golden Mile?'

'Wait.'

She came round to stand in front of his desk. 'For what?'

'For the evidence to be compiled. Once I am clear as to who was involved and to what extent, I will act.' He looked up. It was a statement of fact. He *would* act. In his own time, in his own way.

He intended to see the Beaufort Stud was put out of business. Anthony Lovell, Duke of Missenden, with it. He would send aftershocks through the entire racing fraternity. And if Polly was part of that…

'Don't let your pride hurt the innocent,' Bahiyaa said

softly, moving towards the door. 'Be very certain where your anger is coming from.'

Rashid watched as his sister left and, for a few moments after the door shut, stayed looking at the closed door. Bahiyaa's meaning was clear. She knew how betrayal affected him. Betrayal touched a nerve that had been left exposed during his childhood.

In among the fiasco that was Golden Mile there was betrayal in plenty. People close to him. People he employed and trusted. Under those circumstances how certain was he the cool, clear logic he prided himself on remained the guiding principle of his actions?

But did it matter? If Polly was as innocent of all involvement as Bahiyaa believed her to be it wouldn't matter her visit here was closely supervised. She would get her documentary. He…would get peace of mind.

He pulled a hand across his face.

Only…

Only he'd *kissed* her. And he could still taste her sweetness in his mouth, feel the pressure of her lips on his. A kiss was nothing. He'd kissed many women, enjoyed their company and taken them to bed.

But…

It had been a long time since he'd connected to… He'd been going to say 'a woman', but the truth was it had been a very long time since he'd allowed himself to connect to anyone. And he knew why that was.

Rashid tapped his pen on the table, waiting. His eyes flicked to his wristwatch. Hanif had yet to return his call—and the wait was hard. While his father still lived there was hope of forgiveness, a chance to heal the hurts. Bahiyaa coped so much better than he did. Perhaps because she had long since ceased to seek her father's approval.

At last the phone rang. 'Rashid.'

'No news to report.' His brother's voice sounded weary. 'He is sleeping a great deal. Talking less.'

'Has he asked for…the family to be gathered?'

He'd chosen his words carefully, but Hanif understood the question. 'I'm sorry, Rashid. There has been no change. Not towards you or Bahiyaa, and I have tried.'

Rashid didn't doubt that. His brother would have done everything possible. He sat back in his chair and stared up at the ceiling.

'He really only wants Raiyah, who would prefer not to be here. Samira makes a duty visit twice a day primarily to stake her claim over Raiyah.'

Rashid smiled wryly at the thought of his brother standing between their father's two wives.

'And I've yet to persuade our grandfather he needs to leave Dholar. It's been one nightmare of a day…'

'Anyone know why we're here?' Pete asked, his shirt damp in places from having dragged it on after an interrupted swim.

John shook his head. 'Something's happened. Please God it's not that Crown Prince Khalid has died. If Amrah goes into mourning, then starts to squabble over the old King's successor, we'll be stuffed.'

Polly sipped mint tea, too sweet for her taste, as Pete came to sit beside her. 'You okay?'

She nodded. There was no time for more. Echoing footsteps and the sound of voices heralded the arrival of Rashid. She'd had a long sleepless night to prepare for this moment. Most of the morning. She was ready. Or thought she was.

'Your Highness—' John began, getting to his feet.

Rashid brushed him aside. 'Please sit.'

Polly knew the moment he saw her. It was a fleeting glance but she knew he'd remembered it all. Their conversation in the garden. Their kiss. It was there as a sudden flare in his eyes and she knew hers responded.

What would have happened if she hadn't pulled back? Would they be lovers now? Would she know what he looked like naked? Know how his skin felt beneath her fingers?

If only she'd been braver. That was the regret. She might never have the chance again to know what a man like Rashid Al Baha would be like as a lover.

The sensible part of her brain saw no problem with that. He was obviously a highly sexual man and, for him, it would have meant nothing. It was different for her. Her heart and soul went with her body. If she became his lover she would carry him with her the rest of her life.

'I have had to make some changes to your itinerary.'

John made a guttural sound as though he were about to speak. Rashid's blue eyes turned on him and the other man sat back to listen.

'We will be starting in Al-Jalini—' Rashid nodded to an aide who passed out neatly typed sheets '—as opposed to the Atiq Desert.'

'Are we allowed to ask why?' Steve asked in his Texan drawl.

A muscle in Rashid's cheek flexed. It wouldn't take much, Polly knew, for him to answer, 'Because I wish it.' Whatever his reasons were, he didn't like being questioned on them.

'We went to some pains to keep the details of your visit private. Unfortunately it would seem our security measures have been breached and we must make adjustments. Your safety while in Amrah is my responsibility.'

'We'll need to run these changes by the London office,' John said after a cursory glance down at his paper.

'It has been done. But, of course, you will wish to confirm.'

Polly looked from John to Rashid and back again. There seemed to be more passing between the two men than the words they spoke.

'"We?" Are you proposing to accompany us, Your Highness?'

'Certainly as far as Al-Jalini.' His tone was uncompromising. Certainly left no room for debate. 'By then there will be clearer intelligence as to whether I need to be concerned.'

John nodded. 'Thank you.'

'If you have any questions about these amendments, please speak to Karim Al Rahhbi,' he said, indicating the aide who had passed round the papers.

Polly made a show of looking at the new itinerary, but the point that interested her most was that Rashid had decided to accompany them. There'd never been even the faintest suggestion of that. Slightly scarier was the way her stomach seemed to have leapt into her chest cavity at the thought of time with him, whatever the cause.

It must have been something quite significant that prompted a man like Rashid to alter his own plans. No one had asked about that. She saw the surreptitious glances that passed between the men and judged they already had a pretty good idea what was going on.

Only no one had thought to include her and it was beginning to get a long way up her nose. Even at Shelton she wasn't considered a bit of fluff. True, she was new to this business, but she had come with a brain and if something was happening that concerned her safety she really wanted to know what it was.

'I don't have any questions about the amendments,' she said, her voice stopping Rashid from leaving, 'other than

I'd like to know why it matters if people know where we are going. Are we in any danger?'

'No.' Rashid's eyes met hers. 'If you were in any danger I would not allow you to stay.'

They were in a room full of people but he managed to make that sound so unbelievably intimate. He meant 'you' as in the entire team, but what she heard was 'you' as in 'her'. There was something so primeval in the desire to be nurtured.

She'd not reached the career heights she'd once hoped for herself, but she considered herself a woman of the twenty-first century. Perfectly able to take care of herself. Nevertheless it was intoxicating to feel protected.

'Then why does it matter if people are aware of our itinerary?'

'Polly—'

'It is all right.' Rashid cut across Baz's instinctive exclamation.

Polly met his blue eyes once more and waited while Rashid reached his decision. If the men of the team had been told something she hadn't, she wasn't going to let him leave without telling her.

'Come with me.'

She wasn't in the mood for peremptory instructions but she did want answers. For a start she'd be really interested to know why she was kept separate from the rest of her team. Not that they seemed remotely bothered about it. But was that because she was a woman?

While she was prepared to be adaptable and accepting of a culture different from her own, she was *stuffed* if she was going to be sidelined by a Western film crew and a man who was half English whether he liked it or not.

Without looking at her so called 'colleagues', she stood up and followed him.

'You are cross,' he observed as soon as they were out of hearing.

'Irritated. They might not have expected you to change our itinerary but the whole "your safety is my priority" wasn't a surprise to them, was it?'

Rashid smiled.

'So why have I been left out of the loop?'

'Because you fainted and missed that conversation.'

That hadn't been the answer she'd expected. She'd been geared up for a fiery discussion on the role of women. Now, with nothing to fight against, she felt deflated.

He held open the door to what turned out to be his office. The only concessions to their being in Amrah were the marble floors and the carved screens folded back from the windows. That aside it was a seriously high-tech room meant for business. And it was enormous. On the far wall was a large plasma-screen television and in front of that a Western-style sofa, upholstered in dark brown leather, with a tub chair either side of that.

Polly watched silently as he walked over to his desk and pulled a remote control from the top drawer.

'You remember I told you when we spoke in England that yours would be the second documentary made about my country?'

Polly nodded.

He placed a DVD into the machine and stood back. 'This is it. I would like you to see it before we talk.'

'Have the boys seen this?'

'They have.'

She sat on the sofa, her eyes fixed on the plasma screen. Rashid placed the remote control on the edge of his desk and walked round to sit in his chair.

He'd told her the content was offensive, but the initial

shots of Amrah were just beautiful. The camera panned across a landscape studded with volcanic remains, then across an endless vista of giant sand dunes. A strange, un-cluttered landscape and hauntingly beautiful.

A voice-over quoted Wilfred Thesiger and Polly glanced over at Rashid. There was nothing wrong with any of that. He answered the question in her eyes. 'Watch on,' he said.

Polly settled back and by the end of the short pro-gramme she understood exactly what Rashid's objections were. The Amrah they'd presented to the West was one of dogma and extremes. It spoke of a society where women were suppressed and their human rights violated.

It was so unfair. Everything she'd read in preparation for her visit had described a country that was striving to meld all that was wonderful about the East with the best of the West.

She'd admit to being a little confused by some of the customs she'd encountered, the fact that she and Bahiyaa seemed to occupy an entirely different part of the palace from the men was a strange one, but to portray Amrah as they'd done was irresponsible and, as Rashid had said, of-fensive.

She remained silent as he walked over and removed the DVD from the machine and put it away in its case. He looked across at her. 'I can't deny there are factions in our society who are accurately portrayed here. When my great-grandfather first opened Amrah up to the West there was fierce opposition. My grandfather has continued to encourage Western investment and it is well known my father would have carried on in the same vein. There are people who are deeply suspicious of that.'

He switched off the TV.

'I'm so sorry.' She was angry for him. For his country.

And humiliated by the crassness of hers. No wonder Rashid had been so cautious about allowing a Western film crew into his country. What King Abdul-Aalee had done for Amrah had been amazing and should have been celebrated. 'I'd never take part in a programme like that.'

Rashid smiled. He moved to the chair that was at right angles to the sofa she was sitting on.

'I think it's incredible how much has been done in such a short time. The new schools, hospitals, the emphasis on building a solid infrastructure…'

His smile broadened and Polly felt her insides curl up at the edges. She didn't want to feel like this. She preferred the anger. Felt safer with that. 'Minty would never make a programme like that,' she managed, her voice breathy.

'I am sure she would not.' Rashid brought his fingers together and let them rest against his mouth while he watched her.

He'd watched her yesterday, Polly thought, in just the same way. It was as though he was trying to see inside her, trying to understand more than she said with words. Almost as though she were a specimen under a microscope and then, sometimes, the way he looked at her changed. She became a woman and his pupils dilated.

That was when she felt most afraid. She was hopelessly out of her depth with a man like Rashid Al Baha. It felt a lot like she remembered feeling when she'd been swimming in the sea off Cornwall as a child. There were undercurrents she couldn't see tugging at her, taking her in a direction she knew she shouldn't be going.

The trouble was she wanted to go there. Rashid was excitement. Danger.

When he spoke his voice was low and controlled. 'You have come to Amrah at a crossroads for us politically. My father is dying and the country knows it. The only person who is clinging to a belief that he might be spared is my grandfather.'

Polly heard the edge in his voice that told her how much what he was saying *mattered* to him and irrationally she found it mattered to her. She wished she'd not forced this conversation on him. She ought to have followed the others' lead, been glad of the opportunity to be here at all.

'He is steadfastly refusing to name any successor other than my father.' His mouth twisted. 'While I admire his love and loyalty, it does mean the country is left uncertain of its future direction.'

Rashid paused.

'Who will he choose?' Polly ventured after a moment.

'If his objective is to see his work continue he'll choose my elder brother, Hanif. He's long been considered my father's heir.'

Polly moistened her top lip with the tip of her tongue. 'I still don't understand why it matters if people know where we're going.'

'It might not matter. But Hanif stands for conservative liberalism in a country where there are active extremists.' Rashid's eyes held hers, fiercely blue. 'I have always been aware your visit here might be seen as an opportunity to undermine what Hanif is trying to achieve.'

'In what way?'

'His political opponents could use your visit as propaganda. It would be easy to suggest Hanif is nothing more than a puppet of Western governments.'

'I see.'

'More probably they could seek to embarrass us by compromising your safety.'

News programmes she'd seen over the years of Western

journalists being kidnapped suddenly flashed in her mind. She wasn't brave. She didn't feel any great compulsion to 'get a story out there'. At this moment, given the choice, she'd fly straight back home.

'This morning I received the information that your planned itinerary might have been leaked so I have decided on changes. It is a precaution merely.'

'And you're coming with us?' Polly said, casting an uneasy glance in his direction. If it were a 'precaution merely' why would Rashid Al Baha put aside everything else that claimed his time?

'I am responsible for your safety and I will see no harm comes to you. You have my personal guarantee.'

It was the strangest thing, but Polly didn't doubt it. Looking at Rashid, you simply couldn't doubt he'd deliver exactly what he promised. She'd never had anyone in her life make her feel safe.

Not even in childhood. When her father had died she'd been so scared. Within weeks they'd had to move out of their home on the Shelton estate and buy a small terrace house in Shelton itself. Her room had been painted in gloss red and smelt damp and she'd hated it. For months and months she'd cried herself to sleep, but she'd never told her mother.

Not once. Her father had asked her to look after her and she'd done that. Her role had always been to be 'strong'. Long before the accident that put her mother in the wheel-chair. She was still doing it.

But with Rashid Polly felt she could give over control. She looked at his blue eyes and her initial fear receded. He would keep them safe. *Her* safe.

'Are you happy to continue?'

'Of course,' she answered quickly. 'Will we still leave tomorrow?'

'Unless I hear anything which gives me cause for concern.'

'And if you do?'

'I will send you home.'

He stood up and Polly felt compelled to do the same. Their interview was over and he no doubt had much to do. 'How do I get back to rejoin the others?'

'Do you wish to?'

Heat rippled through her. It would certainly be the safest option but, no, she didn't want to. He was an irresistible temptation. The feeling of being on the edge, of not quite knowing what he was thinking and feeling about her was addictive.

'You haven't had a chance to see Elizabeth's garden in daylight. It would be a shame not to. I could show you now.'

Why was he doing his? Her eyes flicked to his lips. What did he want from her?

'If you have the time, I'd like that.'

No one had ever kissed her as Rashid had last night. Not with that expertise and control. It had been a few seconds of pure sensation before sanity had kicked in. But he was like a drug. He'd awoken her to possibilities, things she really hadn't allowed herself to think. And now he was choosing to spend time with her again.

'I will ask for refreshments to be brought to the summer house.'

'There's a summer house?'

'This garden was designed to soothe Elizabeth's long- ing for home, remember. An English garden must have its summer house. Besides which it provides some welcome shade.' He reached for the phone on his desk and spoke quickly and in Arabic.

This was probably the craziest decision of her entire

life. Polly knew it, but it didn't seem to make any difference.

'That is settled.'

His smile sent shivers coursing through her. A feeling of anticipation. She kept pace as Rashid led her through a maze of corridors. Even if she'd felt at liberty to wander around the palace freely, which she didn't, she wouldn't have had the faintest idea which way to head.

They walked through a Moorish archway and into a formal seating area with low couches. The room was filled with a heady scent that seemed to envelop her. 'What is that smell?'

'*Bokhur.*'

'*Bokhur,*' Polly repeated the unfamiliar word.

Rashid smiled. 'It's incense. Although to say that doesn't communicate its importance to Amrahi households.' He stopped, allowing her to breathe in the complex aroma. 'Every village will have their own *bokhur* maker who will create incense which is unique to that area. The ingredients might be any combination of frankincense, rosewater, sandalwood, ambergris...'

She wrinkled her nose.

'Each recipe is a closely guarded secret, handed down from one generation to the next. And once it is made it is scattered over hot charcoals,' he said, pointing at a silver incense-burner.

It certainly beat the rather bland pot-pourri she placed around the castle, but she wasn't sure she liked it. It was unfamiliar, exotic and slightly cloying as it seemed to seep into the light fabric of her borrowed clothes.

'Do you like it?'

'Perhaps. I'm not sure. It's so different.' But then everything here was so different. *She* was different.

Rashid laughed. 'It is the scent of home.'

She looked at him curiously but, of course, he was right. And for her the 'scent of home' would be newly cut grass, old books and beeswax polish. Nothing as exotic as *bokhur*.

As she went through the doors that led into the garden and into the full heat of the sun she was glad of the co-ordinating *lihaf* Bahiyaa had placed across one shoulder. Deftly, as she'd been shown, Polly placed it over her head.

She looked up and caught Rashid watching her. *Again.* 'It's hot,' she said foolishly.

'And you are fair. You are wise to cover up in the sun.'

Rashid started down one of the paths and, coming into the rose garden from a different direction, Polly immediately saw Elizabeth's summer house. It was open on all sides, more of a pavilion, and smothered in rambling roses.

Elizabeth's summer house. Built for her by a man who had loved her.

'It's beautiful,' she said softly.

Rashid looked down at her. 'I think so.' He watched as she lifted a hand to shade her eyes from the sun, then turned to look back at the palace.

He truly wanted Polly to like this garden, he realised. He loved her wide-eyed enthusiasm. The feeling he was sharing something with her she would treasure.

From the moment his father had given him this palace as his home the rose garden had been a strange attraction. He'd spent years trying to distance himself from his English heritage, but he'd always been drawn to this garden with its strange melding of East and West.

He felt at home here. Peaceful. And that was the purpose of a garden. A place where you could feel at one with yourself and with your God.

'It's not a very English garden, though,' Polly said, looking out across the orange trees, then up at him. 'Don't exactly run to those back home.'

Bahiyaa must have persuaded her to line her eyes in kohl. A dark smoky line around sparkling eyes that were as blue as his own. She looked as much a hybrid as this garden. In traditional Amrahi clothes, hands covered in an intricate henna pattern, she was the embodiment of a fantasy.

It was no part of his plan now to want to kiss her. He'd brought her here to talk. Only it was hard to remember that when his body responded to her with sharp immediacy. He didn't want to talk. He knew what she felt like, tasted like. He knew how her curves fitted against him, how soft her skin was, the warmth of her breath against his mouth, and he craved that.

He hadn't wanted to like her, didn't want to respond to her, but she drew him in anyway. Like a fly on a cobweb, he was more securely caught the more he struggled against it.

But at what cost? Amrah's future rested on the next few days and he'd been indiscreet in what he'd told her earlier. The knowledge that negative publicity would harm Hanif was power if she chose to use it.

He needed to be sure of her reasons for being here. It wasn't enough to believe her innocent. He had to *know*. His feelings for Polly were complicated, but he needed to focus on why he'd arranged for her to stay at his home.

'Fresh oranges still warm from the sun is about as far from a frost-bitten February day as you can get. Even if we manage to restore the orangery we'll never be able to recreate anything like this at Shelton.'

'But it's not a traditional Amrahi garden either,' Rashid countered, watching the sunlight catch at the silver embroidery that edged her *lihaf*, 'although it has elements you'd expect to find in one. The fountain, the long rills of water… Even the simplest Arab garden finds space for water.'

'It's beautiful,' Polly said, looking up at him.

She was happy now. *With him.* If he kissed her now would she stop him as she had yesterday or would she surrender to the inevitable? Because in any other place, at any other time, it would have been inevitable.

'English gardens have fountains, too. At Shelton we have a spectacular one which you can see from the Summer Sitting Room.'

The mention of her stepbrother's ancestral home was as effective as a cold shower. Did Polly know the extent to which Anthony Lovell had borrowed against his inheritance? Quite possibly selling Golden Mile to Rashid had been the last act of a very desperate man.

And desperate men could be very persuasive. And maybe her love for the house was enough of a temptation. Without any interference on his part he couldn't see the duke holding on to his country seat for long.

They walked down the vine-shaded path towards the summer house. 'You always speak of Shelton Castle with such affection.'

Polly looked up at him, a warm smile lighting her eyes. 'I love it. I always have. My mother says it's because I've polished most of it. Which is true. I had my first job at the castle at fourteen.'

Rashid said nothing, hoping his silence would encourage her to speak.

'There's such a sense of history about the place. Every nook and cranny could tell you a story. And we have our own resident ghost.'

'You believe that?'

'I've never seen her but there are plenty who will swear to it. We call her the Mad Duchess, but actually she was Lady Margaret Chenies who was married, pretty much against her will, to the very first Duke of Missenden back at the time of the English Civil War.' Her blue eyes danced with mischief.

'Was she mad?'

'Highly strung, I think, and lived a miserable life.'

'As all ghosts should.'

'Certainly.'

Rashid watched, fascinated at the hint of a dimple. 'Lady Margaret was absolutely devoted to her only son who was killed at the Siege of Gloucester in sixteen forty-three and she threw herself out of the window in her grief.'

'Ah.'

'But there are those who say she was pushed by her philandering husband. She now walks the Long Gallery, which actually wasn't built in sixteen forty-three, calling his name.'

Rashid smiled. It was impossible not to. Her enthusiasm for her subject was infectious—as it had been in the documentary on Shelton. She was a natural in front of the camera and it was really not surprising her friend had decided to utilise her talent.

He felt himself weaken a little more. He wanted to believe her, but if he believed her that would lead to a whole new list of problems.

How possible was it to have an affair with a woman whose life you were destroying? When he took Shelton away from her stepbrother what would she do? Would she hate him?

'Do you intend to do more television work after this?'

Polly shook her head. 'I shouldn't think so. I suppose

if it came my way I wouldn't turn it down, but I don't have any great specialism to bring to anything.'

'What do you plan on doing?'

'I'll return to Shelton.'

'Straight away?'

'Well, Easter is the start of the tourist season and there'll be lots to do to get the house ready in time.'

Again that sparkling enthusiasm, but he fancied he saw something else. Something she wasn't saying. Something that clouded her enjoyment of the castle and her role in it.

They stepped up into the summer house and Polly sat down on the intricate seat facing out towards the small ornamental lake. 'How come everything's so green here?'

Rashid sat facing her. 'There is a complex irrigation system in place, all stemming from a natural spring.'

'Created for Elizabeth?'

He nodded, watching the expressions pass over her beautiful face.

'King Mahmoud must have loved her very much,' she said wistfully. 'It was a shame they had to hurt so many people to be together. It spoils the story for me.'

She kept surprising him. That was not a sentiment he'd have expected to hear expressed by an Englishwoman. In his experience they wanted money and power and would achieve that even if the money and power were found in another woman's husband.

Rashid turned to watch the arrival of the servant bringing fruit juices. Two large jugs. One of lime juice and the other of pomegranate.

He looked back at Polly to see she'd taken off her *lihaf* and shaken her blond hair free. It was all too easy to imagine it spread out on a pillow next to him. Far too easy to want it there.

'Do you have a preference between lime and pome-granate?'

'Isn't lime juice sharp?'

'Try it.' He spoke to the servant in clipped Arabic, who then poured two glass of the lime juice, his head respect-fully bowed throughout. It did him enormous credit because the temptation to look at her must have been acute.

If Polly were his he'd want to shield her from every eye but his.

Rashid picked up one of the glasses and sipped. It was dangerous to even think that way. Even if Polly were not related by marriage to the Duke of Missenden she could never play a part in his life. She was as unsuitable a choice as his mother had been for his father.

Destined for disaster. Two cultures that couldn't do anything but clash. It *was* time he decided on a wife, but he wouldn't search for her in the West.

He watched, silently, as Polly took her first sip of lime juice. But all thoughts of finding himself a wife would have to wait. What mattered now was determining if this woman presented a problem to Hanif's succession.

'This is lovely. Really refreshing and clean.' She looked up and smiled. 'My favourite so far.'

It seemed to him her smile filled the garden. 'I'm glad.'

And then there was silence. A faint breeze caught at her shimmering blond hair, a hennaed hand reaching out to brush one wayward strand off her pale cheek.

'I can't imagine ever wanting to leave somewhere so beautiful—especially if it had been created for me.'

There wasn't a movement Polly made that didn't feel erotic. Rashid felt as though his skin had suddenly become two sizes too small for his body.

'Why did she leave here?'

He forced his eyes to scan the sweet-smelling flowers that scrambled through the trees. Anywhere but look at her and her wide-eyed sensual beauty. 'She didn't have the choice. Their love affair was a scandal here, too.'

'Because King Mahmoud was married?'

'He had only two wives when he met Elizabeth and could easily have afforded a third,' Rashid said with a shake of his head. 'The problem was that she was not free to make a commitment to him.'

'But if she hadn't been married that would have been fine?'

He nodded.

Polly pursed her lips. 'There's something wrong with that. Why would any woman agree to marry a man who already had two wives?'

He'd had this conversation many, many times during his years at Cambridge University. Beyond anything else it was the thing that touched a nerve in Western women and he'd come to enjoy the debate.

'Perhaps a woman who trusts her father,' he said, sitting back, watching her face.

It wasn't what he wanted for himself. He wanted a woman who would entrance him all his days, an equal, one who would protect and care for his children with her life, a woman who would love him and only him.

'In my culture a man's wife is chosen by his family, taking into account his status, family background and intellectual capacity.'

'How romantic!'

'The husband and wife bring a shared sense of values and an understanding of duty. Romantic love often comes later.'

'And if it doesn't,' Polly said, her eyes watching him from over the rim of her fruit juice, 'he just gets himself another wife!'

She knew he was enjoying himself at her expense and the teasing glint in her eyes was irresistible. Rashid smiled. 'It is not quite as simple as you make it sound. While a man is permitted up to four wives, I know none of my generation who would choose to do so. Each wife must be treated equally...in all things.

'Had King Mahmoud married Elizabeth he would have needed to create two more gardens as beautiful as this one for his other wives. A man with more than one wife must share his time, his body and his possessions equally. Expensive and physically exhausting, I'm sure you'll agree.'

Rashid sat back and watched the blush that spread across Polly's cheekbones. He couldn't remember the last time he'd seen a woman blush. No Amrahi woman was left alone with him long enough for that to be a possibility and he'd thought Englishwomen had forgotten how to.

'And all rather silly if he can have a mistress anyway.'

'Ah, but that is human frailty at work, not a guiding principle.'

Polly laughed, seemingly because she couldn't help it. Warmth spiralled out in a coil from the pit of his stomach.

'So, will you marry the woman your family chooses?'

There was the difficult question, the one he'd prefer not to answer. He saw the advantages played out all around him, but the honest answer was 'no'. How could he? To marry a woman of your family's choosing required confidence in their ability to choose wisely and with your happiness in mind.

His father and grandfather were remarkable men, men who had achieved great things in the time allotted to them on earth, but he did not trust their judgement.

'When the time comes,' Rashid said firmly, 'I will choose my own wife.'

CHAPTER SIX

'AND Bahiyaa?' Polly asked. 'Will she get to choose her own husband?'

'Bahiyaa is already married. But, the answer to your question is that my sister's marriage was arranged by our father and approved of by my grandfather.'

Polly frowned. There'd not been a whisper of that. Not in all the conversations she'd had with his sister. And Rashid's manner had changed, his jaw was set and his cheekbones flushed.

'Have I met him?'

Rashid shook his head. 'Bahiyaa's marriage was particularly unsuccessful. Eventually she made the decision to leave her husband and seek sanctuary with her own family.'

'But she's not divorced?'

'Her husband doesn't wish it,' he stated bluntly. And then, as though he realised she would need more explanation that that, 'In Amrah a divorce is not an automatic right. Bahiyaa must convince a court she has sufficient grounds. Omeir is an intelligent and articulate man who has been very convincing. And our mistake was not realising soon enough her husband would refuse to let her go.

She has no way now of substantiating her version of events.'

Shock held Polly silent, for a moment. 'And that's it? There's nothing she can do?'

'For the time being.'

It was unfair to push him any further, but she really wanted to know. Not merely from idle curiosity, although she had to admit there was something of that, too, but because she cared about Bahiyaa. Sometimes, when his sister hadn't known she was being watched she'd looked so sad.

The kind of sad that went beyond emotion. Much as her mother had been in the first few months after her father had died. And, being a natural 'fixer', she'd wondered what she could do to help. She'd not imagined anything like this, though.

'Even with a family as influential as yours? Surely if your grandfather intervened on her—'

'Even so.'

Polly let her finger slowly trace the rim of her glass. 'How long has Bahiyaa lived apart from her husband?'

'Four years.'

'*Four?*'

Rashid held up his hand as though to silence her. 'I know. There is huge injustice in what is happening to Bahiyaa. I feel it deeply.' He took another sip of his fruit juice and appeared to be lost in thought.

He sighed. 'When a man takes a wife,' Rashid said quietly, 'our religion teaches us it is a uniting of souls for all of eternity. It is the husband's duty to love and care for his wife throughout her life.'

Put like that it was beautiful. The Christian marriage ceremony was the same. 'To love and to cherish in sickness and health.' So often people didn't manage to live up to those vows, but it was a great starting point.

'And it wasn't like that for Bahiyaa?'

'No.' Rashid's voice took on the steely quality she'd often heard in it. 'Omeir is an influential man from a good family. He's gifted in many areas, but he is also cruel and violent.'

'Violent?'

'To give my father his due I sincerely believe he had no idea when he brokered that marriage.'

Polly sat in stunned silence. Bahiyaa was so lovely. Intelligent, warm and stunningly beautiful. What more could a man want in a wife?

'Of course, Bahiyaa did her best. She is a strong woman and she wanted her marriage to be a success. Its failure has caused her to experience a shame I do not believe she should feel. She was also, rightly as it turned out, not sure of our father's support.'

'Why ever not?' The question shot from Polly's mouth without any thought.

'It is a question of honour. Our family's honour.'

'That doesn't make any sense. *He* was divorced.'

'It is different for a man.'

'It shouldn't be!'

'And my mother is English.' Rashid allowed himself a tight smile, the skin across his cheekbones pulled tight. 'She did not consider herself bound by the precepts of a religion not her own. And I will own she had the full support of her own family.'

But she'd left her son behind. Polly couldn't imagine the pain of that. Whatever had compelled Rashid's mother to do that? He'd spoken of having chosen to be Arab. Perhaps he'd been put in the impossible position of having to choose between parents?

It was a little like treading on eggshells, but she had to ask. 'Did she have to leave Amrah without you?'

'Certainly. She didn't have the legal right to take me without my father's permission and he would never have given it. Perhaps if I'd been a daughter… But even then, I don't think so. By the time she left it would have been as much about punishment as legal right.'

A lump filled her throat. More than a century before Elizabeth Lewis had chosen to leave her child, too, and there'd been such heartache in the wake of that decision. Rashid might give the impression of being invincible, but it was the ultimate rejection.

Polly moistened her lips. 'What made her leave?'

'It is no secret.' Rashid refilled his glass with lime juice and silently offered to refill hers.

She nodded. 'Please.'

'Put simply, my father wished to take a second wife.' He allowed himself a very small smile. 'You will not be surprised to learn my mother objected.'

'Polygamy is not an English concept. He must have known that.'

Rashid placed the jug back down on the tray. 'Indeed. But my father's desire to have a junior wife was predominantly motivated by political necessity and, no doubt, emotional blackmail. My grandfather wished it.'

She sat in silence but, honestly, she couldn't comprehend of any situation that would justify what Rashid's father had done to a woman he'd presumably married for love. *And to his son.*

He'd robbed his young son of his mother. She didn't know what to say. Probably because there was nothing that could be said. The hurts were there, scar tissue covering wounds that had imperfectly healed.

'It was political. In the early years of my grandfather's

reign he favoured his much younger brother, Prince Faisal, as his successor. That was a sensible choice.

'But time passed, and by the grace of God my grandfather lived a long and fruitful life. Eventually it became logical to choose an heir from among his own nine sons.' Rashid picked up his glass, swirling the fruit juice around as though it were whisky.

Polly waited while he sipped. The whole concept of senior and junior wives was alien to her. Having nine sons was unusual. Needing to name one as a successor more unusual still.

But it was his pain that held her silent. He related facts as though they were no more than that, but his features were set like granite.

'My father is the eldest. At the time he was in his mid thirties, a highly educated man, disciplined, popular with the Amrahi people, and already the father of two sons. You would think an obvious choice, but my grandfather was, *is*,' Rashid amended, 'adamant that Amrah's sovereign be entirely of Arab blood.'

It was like being given a key to his soul. So much about Rashid was falling into place. Polly felt such anger. She didn't think she'd ever experienced anything quite as intense. At eight years old this strong, beautiful man had been made to feel he would never be good enough by the people whose business it was to love and care for him.

Rashid stared out across the lake for a few moments. 'Princess Yasmeen, my father's first wife, and the woman my grandfather had selected as a suitable bride, had died young. I assume my father was sincerely attached to her because he refused to contemplate a second marriage.'

'Until he met your mother.' Polly knew what was coming next. She understood. Hanif was a suitable heir. He, Rashid, was not.

'I can't imagine my grandfather was happy about it but my father married her anyway. If he'd thought my grandfather would soften his views, he was wrong.'

Polly blinked hard against the tears prickling behind her eyes.

'Remember Amrah was a young country, newly emerging from a century of isolation. My grandfather was spearheading rapid modernisation and surrounded by voices counselling caution in his choice of successor.'

Rashid's voice grew more distant. 'If anything happened to Hanif they feared my father might be tempted to name me as the future king and gave him an ultimatum. He needed to take a second bride.'

'Could he have refused?'

'He could.' Rashid brought his eyes back to hers. 'He was a grown man. But my grandfather knew he wouldn't. One of my father's strengths is his love and commitment to Amrah. Although my grandfather rightly receives much of the credit for the skilful blend of tradition and modernity here, I think history will recognise my father's contribution.'

For the first time Rashid's voice held a trace of an emotion other than hurt. *Pride.* Crown Prince Khalid might be many things, but he was clearly a father Rashid had looked up to. Loved. Still loved?

She studied him. It was inconceivable that any father wouldn't have delighted in a son like Rashid.

Or grandfather.

King Abdullah had wilfully ripped a young family apart. And Rashid's father had let him.

'There is a history of rebellion in the Muzna region and it was suggested that ties could be strengthened if my father married Sheikh Sulaiman's eldest daughter, Samira.'

There was a hideous logic, but what of Samira? It was hateful for her. 'Did she agree?'

'She was seventeen at the time, offered the chance to become a princess…'

And she'd thought life at Shelton was complicated.

'Within weeks of that marriage my mother returned to England.'

Leaving Rashid behind to be brought up by the woman who'd replaced her. 'That's incredibly sad.'

'As you say,' he conceded.

It was more than sad. It was heartbreaking. For them both. 'Did you see her? Growing up?'

'No.'

Her heart felt so unbearably heavy.

'As a child I only knew she'd chosen to leave. I never questioned my father's judgement.'

'And do you see her now?' she asked, her voice husky.

'Occasionally. She is my mother. I respect her as my mother but I have chosen to embrace the life she rejected.' His voice was, once again, devoid of all emotion. 'There is no fairy-tale ending. She is a woman I barely know.'

Polly stared out across the ornamental lake towards the orange trees, looking but not seeing. 'Did she marry again?'

'Yes.'

'And had more children?' Polly pushed.

'I have two half-sisters. Miranda and Portia.'

Two English sisters. Half-sisters he scarcely knew.

'And Princess Samira and your father have had children together, haven't they?'

'Three sons and five daughters. More recently my father decided to take a junior wife and Princess Raiyah gave birth to twin sons a little over two years ago.'

'So, what's that?' Polly frowned, mentally counting

through Rashid's family. 'Seven sons. Your grandfather must be delighted his plan worked so well,' she said acerbically.

King Abdullah seemed like a Machiavellian puppeteer, pulling the strings of those around him. And Rashid's father a victim of his own ambition. She couldn't like that any more than she liked Elizabeth Lewis's selfishness.

Other people mattered. They *did*. For the first time in six years she was suddenly hugely grateful she understood that. There was nothing more important than the people you loved. The years she'd spent at Shelton seemed years very well spent.

'Except my grandfather is likely to outlive my father. He will need to name a new heir and Samira's eldest son is still young.'

So all that upheaval and heartache might have been for nothing. Crown Prince Khalid was not going to live long enough to be King and his sons might not inherit either. One would have thought, having lived through that, he'd have been more receptive to his daughter's situation.

'What made Bahiyaa take the decision to finally leave her husband?'

The muscle in Rashid's cheek worked painfully. 'Omeir had never left a mark on Bahiyaa where it could be seen, but on that night he threw her against a wall and she broke her wrist putting her hands up to break her fall. When she came to me she had a black eye, bruising to her face and marks around her neck.'

Deep loathing washed over Polly in unstoppable waves. She'd only known Bahiyaa for such a short time but imagining her in that situation brought such revulsion. Thank God she'd had the courage to leave at last. Even in England, where divorce held no stigma, she knew women so often found it hard.

'Three weeks later she lost the baby she'd been carrying.'

Oh, dear God, no! Polly reached out instinctively, her hand lightly touching his. 'She was lucky to have somewhere to come.'

His fingers closed around hers, dark against the paleness of her skin. 'She lives under my protection. She's safe, but she has lost so much. The possibility of children. Companionship.'

Love, Polly added silently. If ever there was a woman capable of loving it was Bahiyaa. 'Couldn't…?' She stared down at their joined hands. 'Couldn't your father do something to help her?'

'He refuses even to see her.'

'Even now?' Polly couldn't keep the shock from her voice. Crown Prince Khalid was dying. Surely *now*, when he realised how short a time he had left, he'd want to see his daughter. Make things safe for her.

'He is adamant Bahiyaa should return to her husband.'

'And be beaten?'

'I have to believe he doesn't think that will happen.'

Her hand moved against his. Of course, he had to believe his father was acting out of ignorance. How could you have any respect left for a man who would allow his daughter to live in fear, particularly when she'd had the courage to ask for help?

It must be doubly painful if that man was someone you'd spent your entire life revering.

'How long is your father expected to live?'

Rashid shrugged. 'Hours. Days. Weeks. His cancer is advanced but he is a strong man. It will take the time it takes.'

And he was going to die without telling his daughter how much he loved her.

She'd been so lucky. Her father had left nothing unsaid. She'd never been in doubt he'd gone away from them only because he'd had to. And that had carried her. Always.

'She seems so calm.'

'She is accepting. I think she's reached the point where she is content not to live in fear. I find the separation from our father more difficult.'

Polly looked up. She hadn't understood that by taking Bahiyaa in Rashid had broken contact with his father, too. That conversation back in Minty's office about why Rashid wasn't doing the 'bedside vigil thing' suddenly seemed glib.

He wasn't there because he wasn't allowed to be there.

Never had Rashid seemed quite so human. Or so desirable. He'd made a conscious decision to do the right thing at enormous personal cost. He was all that was standing between his sister and an unthinkable future.

A strong, sexy, wonderful man. A man you could trust. A man worth loving. Polly's gaze drifted to Rashid's mouth and the lips that had kissed her. She studied the curve of them, the fullness of his bottom lip as compared to the top one. The cleft in his chin.

'Polly.'

From somewhere deep inside her a tear welled up and rolled slowly down her cheek. She wasn't sure why exactly. Whether she was crying for the boy Rashid had been, the man he was now or for Bahiyaa, she couldn't tell. She only knew she felt an overwhelming sense of sadness flow through her.

Rashid moved. He sat beside her and his left hand moved to brush her hair off her face, his thumb coming back to wipe away the moisture on her cheek. His face so close to hers. She could feel his fingers skim her neck. But it was his eyes that caused heat to lick along her limbs.

She wanted him with a passion she really didn't understand. It was a compulsion. A *need*. Something that transcended morality and sense. It wasn't even really about sex. It was about belonging. About recognising that this was the man she'd been waiting for.

'You're so beautiful.'

Incredibly, with the truth of that burning in his blue eyes, she felt beautiful. His hand brushed her cheek, setting the long gold earrings Bahiyaa had given her swinging. She felt them touch her neck.

It seemed such a long time before he lowered his mouth to hers. Every millisecond she was urging him on, willing him to kiss her with all the passion she knew he was capable of.

Rashid's hands cradled her face and his mouth was hard against hers. His kiss was everything it had been yesterday and more. There was desperation in it, a certain knowledge that this passion was beyond wisdom. They lived lives so very far apart. There could be no future. Nothing more than this moment.

But this moment was all she wanted. Heat coursed through her veins and settled in the pit of her stomach. She was beyond excitement.

I want him. The words pounded in her head with each beat of her heart. *I want him to love me.*

His tongue moved against her mouth. The lightest touch on her lips and she heard her own gasp for breath. She wanted to taste him. Feel him invade her body. Her lips parted and her heart thudded against her breasts.

Rashid's hand moved round to the small of her back urging her closer, his left hand tilting her face to allow him maximum access.

There was nothing she wouldn't do for him. *Nothing.* Here, *now*, in Elizabeth's garden, she'd be his lover if that was what he wanted. She only wanted his lips to go on kissing her. Kissing her until she was certain there was no life outside this moment.

Her whole body was humming with a pleasure, a hot ache low in her abdomen. She needed more. Wanted more.

The sound of smashing glass barely pierced her consciousness, but Rashid pulled back, his breathing uneven.

She moaned.

'Your glass,' he said roughly.

No. Inside she was screaming, but her pride kicked in. She ignored the lime juice spread out over the summer-house floor and bent down to collect slivers of glass in the palm of her hand.

Rashid touched her hair. 'Leave it.'

She placed what she'd gathered already in one neat pile and looked up, knowing that he'd remembered all the reasons why kissing her wasn't a good idea.

'You are too beautiful to resist.'

No one had ever said that to her. It warmed her even as she knew what he was really saying. 'Too beautiful' meant that kiss shouldn't have happened.

The girl she'd been back in England would have agreed. It *was* foolish. She was no more suitable a bride for Rashid Al Baha than his mother had been for his father. She could only be a temporary distraction and if she continued down this path she'd be hurt.

Desperately hurt. For whatever reason Rashid had let her glimpse behind the mask. She knew what motivated him, what had shaped him. She saw more than perhaps even he'd intended.

And she ached to have his arms around her once more. The future didn't seem so very important any more. It would take care of itself and if all she could have were memories she'd settle for those.

Rashid brushed his thumb against her swollen lips and then, with his eyes holding hers, he placed her *lihaf* over her head. 'The heat of the sun is fierce now. I ought to take you back inside.'

Away from him. *Away from temptation.*

'Thank you for telling me about your father. And about Bahiyaa.' Polly tugged at the side of her bottom lip with her teeth in an effort not to cry. 'She is fortunate to have a brother like you.'

It took immense courage to turn away, but she did it. Head high, she stepped down out of the summer house and into the midday sun. Heat seemed to rise up from the marble paving in waves, her legs brushing against the sweet-smelling herbs that spilled out across the warm stone.

'Polly.'

She forced her feet to slow. If her smile was a little too bright it was unlikely Rashid would notice. She turned and waited for him to catch up. 'Which way now? Will the guys still be in the *Majlis*?'

'Quite possibly. Is that where you wish to go?'

No, it wasn't. The thought of having to make small talk with people she scarcely knew didn't appeal in the slightest. What she wanted was solitude and the chance to mull over what Rashid had told her. A chance, too, to understand what was happening to her. 'I think I might like to read for a while.'

Rashid nodded. 'Then I shall take you to find Bahiyaa. She will show you the way to your room.'

It had always been a matter of 'when' not 'if' Bahiyaa would track him down. Not because he imagined Polly would have referred to his sister's unhappy marriage or that Bahiyaa would mind if she had, but because she had become their guest's champion.

Perhaps it was because she was wrongly judged herself she felt a need to protect Polly from what she saw as an unjust accusation? Perhaps it was nothing more than friendship? While Omeir and their father remained intransigent, her life was necessarily secluded and she must often be lonely.

'Polly…'

Rashid saved the work on his computer and gave his sister his full attention.

'Have you reached any conclusions?'

He supposed he must have.

Inadvertently. Nothing about this morning had gone to plan. The questions he had about her stepbrother and her life at Shelton had remained unasked, but it seemed he'd reached a decision all the same.

Rashid rubbed a hand around the back of his neck. He hadn't intended to kiss Polly for a second time any more than he'd intended to bare his soul. But her beautiful moist eyes, her hand in his, and he'd been unable to resist her.

The sweetness of her kiss seemed to reach deep inside him and grab hold of his heart. He'd felt her vulnerability to him and it had enflamed him. What troubled him was the sense of intimacy he felt.

That was new.

He didn't do intimacy. Rashid picked up his fountain pen and twisted it between thumb and forefinger. He liked to play fair. His relationships had always been about sex, need, passion, wanting…

They were not based on conversation. No woman he'd ever slept with had imagined she would occupy a permanent place in his life. If he felt they were getting too close he stepped back.

But Polly had crossed some kind of line. And he didn't

want that. His family's privacy was sacrosanct and yet, for some reason, he'd felt able to talk to her. And, having done so, he trusted her not to use that information to hurt the people he loved.

That had to be his decision. He trusted her. When he looked into her blue eyes he saw honesty—which meant she was going to be hurt.

Because of him.

Rashid glanced across at his sister, who was looking at him with a slight knowing smile.

'She knows nothing, Rashid.'

He pushed his chair back from his desk. 'Perhaps.'

'I have had so many conversations about her life at Shelton Castle. I do not think she cares for her stepbrother at all.'

'He is a thoroughly unpleasant man.'

'She says "weak".'

'That would be right.' Weak, greedy and dishonest. But he was her family, if only by marriage. 'If she dislikes him so much, has she told you why she stays?'

'Because of her mother's accident.'

Bahiyaa twisted the gold bangles on her wrist. 'And have you thought to ask her what her stepbrothers felt about their father's remarriage? What they said?' She moved closer. 'Have you asked her what she fears will be Shelton's future?'

Rashid moved his pen from one hand to the other and back again, twisting it all the time between long, lean fingers.

She smiled. 'I am wondering, Rashid, what you have been talking about for so long. You seem to have discovered very little.'

Her dark, kohl-lined eyes smiled understandingly across the distance between them.

'Surely it would be simplest to ask her about Golden Mile?'

'It need not concern her.'

'Of course it will concern her! Shelton Castle is her home and a place she loves. She has poured her life into it and what you propose to do will rip it from her. You cannot destroy the Duke of Missenden without hurting Polly. And,' Bahiyaa continued with unaccustomed force, 'you are working towards that end while offering her friendship. I do not think she will be able to forgive you that, Rashid. And I'm not sure you will forgive yourself.'

'My honour demands justice.'

'You have the power to temper your justice with mercy if you so choose. Rashid, I *know* you.' Her hennaed hand reached out and touched his arm. 'You will never be content with a girl who has lived her entire life in Amrah. You say that is what you—'

Rashid moved abruptly and set his pen down on the desk. Bahiyaa was hitting too close to home, touching a nerve that was newly exposed. 'When I marry I will choose a girl from my own culture. I will look for the mother of my children.'

'You should choose the woman you love,' Bahiyaa corrected softly. 'And if you love wisely she will be a woman who can help you accept that two cultures have shaped you, Rashid. And your children will be blessed because they have parents who will nurture them in a loving relationship.'

He saw her blink hard. 'You, Hanif and I did not have that. What we experienced was not good.'

What she had experienced in her own marriage had been infinitely worse, Rashid added silently.

CHAPTER SEVEN

RASHID was ready to leave for Al-Jalini long before the appointed early start. Long before the plaintive wail of the muezzin drifted out across Samaah, calling the faithful to prayer.

He'd slept fitfully. Bahiyaa's words had burned deep inside him—as she had intended they should. It was as though she'd held up a mirror to his life and forced him to take a good hard look at it. And having taken a look he wasn't so sure he liked what he saw.

He was still that boy trying to fit in, trying to find acceptance, trying to be better, stronger, make things *right*. Rashid swore softly.

Because he'd known his father was watching for signs of his mother, he'd subjugated everything he could about himself that would remind him of her. And he'd tried to make his father proud of him. He'd rode faster than Hanif, on horses that his brother wouldn't have ventured near. He'd learnt swathes of Amrahi history. Even his love of the desert had been born out of his burning need for acceptance.

But whatever he'd done had never been enough. It was time to accept that and understand why. He had his mother's eyes and, when his father looked at him, he saw her. The woman who had publicly shamed him. There'd been no way back from that.

And in the way of a child he'd come to loathe what he had been told was loathsome. Bahiyaa was right. He needed to come to terms with the fact two cultures had shaped the man he'd become and find a way of balancing them within himself.

Bahiyaa had spoken, too, of his taking a wife. It was time. He yearned for family. To create what he had never really had.

Over the years he and Hanif had spent many hours teasing each other over their father's choice of prospective brides. A second cousin. The daughter of an influential sheikh on whose land there was oil. They'd resisted. Always.

But, when the time came, Hanif would do his duty. His brother knew, and had always known, there was no reason to suppose their grandfather would not place the same stipulations on him as he had on his own son. It was his destiny to marry dynastically and Hanif had accepted it.

His brother would respect the woman his family chose and he would probably be happy. He would derive solace from his children and would pour his energies into the environmental issues that so concerned him. And should his grandfather decide to make him his successor, he would devote the last breath of his body to Amrah and its people.

Rashid's own future path was less well delineated. His choices wider. But he feared Bahiyaa was right. He would not be satisfied by a relationship based on duty and friendship.

He had told Polly he would choose his own bride and he stood by that. He, and only he, would determine what would best suit him in a wife. And what would suit him was a woman who understood he was an Arab at heart.

However he'd come to it, Amrah was the place his soul felt at peace. It was foolishness to suppose a woman brought up with the freedoms of the West would live happily here and that must guide his choice.

It could not, *would* not, be a woman like Polly.

He turned his head at Karim's tap on the door. His aide held the papers he'd been waiting for.

'Everything you asked for is here, Prince Rashid.'

Rashid nodded. 'Leave the file on my desk.' He turned back to fill his lungs with the early morning air, looking out across the courtyard garden.

His feelings about Polly were complicated. Bahiyaa, despite it all, was a romantic, but even she had counselled he 'love wisely'.

'Wisely' could not mean loving a woman who was related by marriage to a man he would ruin. And he *would* have justice. Bahiyaa didn't understand that not to would lay him open to ridicule throughout the racing world. His actions would be moderate but decisive. Not revenge. Justice.

He would also act to minimise the consequences to both Polly and her mother. That was the act of an honourable man.

With no real appetite for the job at hand, Rashid sat himself at his desk and worked his way through the latest developments in their investigation. Written confirmation of what he'd already been told verbally. His agent admitted accepting payment from the Duke of Missenden.

The betrayal of a man he'd considered a close friend had wounded him deeply, but his way was clear. With immense regret he would instruct Karim to make the necessary phone calls. Quietly he would let it be known Farid had forged documentation. He would never be in a position where he could accept a bribe again.

And it saddened Rashid.

As did the details of how Shelton was run, where the day-to-day finance of the castle came from, how many staff were employed on the estate...

What was clear was that Karim's request for the money paid for Golden Mile to be returned could only happen if the Duke of Missenden sold Shelton Castle. And only if he was given a very generous deadline to meet his obligation.

Everything Polly had worked for would be lost. It would be little consolation to her to know it was the consequence of her stepbrother's actions when it was his hand that wielded the justice.

Rashid shut the file and placed a stick-it note on the top, writing '*Action*. Proceed as arranged' in his usual bold hand.

He had no choice, but it was the strangest feeling. He'd finally got the evidence he'd been waiting for, he'd given the instruction to proceed and yet he felt no sense of peace about it. No satisfaction.

And the reason for that was Polly.

Not only had they not turned up anything that incriminated her, they had referred to her as Shelton's 'salvation'. Without her input it seemed her stepbrother would have lost the castle eighteen months ago.

She was the chatelaine of the castle. It was her strength of character that took a skeleton staff and made it possible to host evenings like the one he'd first seen her at.

Sulaiman, one of his most trusted staff members, came in with a low bow. 'Your guests are ready to leave, Your Highness.'

He stood immediately. Surely, Polly would agree he had a right to seek redress for a multimillion-pound fraud perpetrated against him?

But Bahiyaa had hit home. He *had* lied to Polly by omission. And he *was* going to take away something she'd devoted years of her life to. By the time she returned to England her life would have been altered in a way she could never have expected.

Rashid stepped out into the bright sunshine and immediately saw Polly standing a little away from the rest of her team, her hand shading her eyes, looking up at the vast doors to the palace. Just as she'd stood looking out across the rose garden.

She seemed to sense him because she turned and smiled. Involuntarily he walked towards her.

'Karim says we are not permitted to take photographs of the palace. Are you sure about that?'

'Quite sure.'

'Really?'

'It is my home and, therefore, private.'

'Shelton Castle is my home and we allow people to take photographs all the time.'

Guilt washed through him. He needed to tell her everything, but he wanted to do so in a way that would soften the blow.

He liked her. He admired her strength.

And for all he'd told himself he would keep his distance from her he still wanted to kiss her. If he'd been able to he would have held her close and shielded her from life's blows with his own body.

She looked very different from the woman in the rose garden. Her face was clear of make-up, her blond hair secured in a single braid and her clothes were Western. Very much more the woman he'd first met at Shelton.

He wanted to kiss beneath her ear lobe and down the length of her neck to where her clavicle met her collarbone. Run his tongue along her bottom lip, coaxing, teasing…

Beyond foolish. Rashid moved away, walking towards the waiting cars.

Baz looked up from the maps he'd laid out across the bonnet. 'Will we be taking the main coast road?'

He was deliberately slow to answer, and grateful when Steve sauntered over to ask, 'How long a drive? It looks like it'll take the best part of the day.'

Another lie by omission. At least this one was to ensure their safety.

'Your Highness,' Karim interrupted, 'there is a telephone call I think you should take.'

A chill spread through him like ink through water. Rashid forced himself to swallow, finding his voice. 'I apologise. I will be the shortest possible time.' Abruptly he turned on his heel and walked back inside.

Karim kept pace. 'It is His Highness Prince Hanif, Your Highness.'

He nodded, his emotions held taut. Rashid reached across his desk and picked up the receiver. 'What news?'

His brother equally wasted no time. 'I've just spoken to the consultant oncologist and we're talking days. His kidneys have failed.'

It was news he'd been expecting, but it didn't make hearing it any easier. *Days.* Rashid looked up to see Bahiyaa standing in the doorway. 'Is he still able to hold a conversation?' he asked, his eyes watching for his sister's reaction to his question.

'Sporadically. He is taking large doses of morphine and is sleeping most of the time.'

'Has he—?' Rashid began.

'No.'

No. He still refused to see Bahiyaa.

'And I think we have passed the point we might have expected it.'

Rashid shook his head at his sister and she nodded. She had no tears left to cry and that ripped him apart. All that was left was acceptance.

'Rashid, do you want to be here at the end? I'm sure he could be persuaded to see you. Or at the very least you could be sent for as soon as he slips into unconsciousness...'

His hand gripped the receiver until his knuckles showed white. What was the point of that? He could watch his father take his last breath—but only as long as his father wasn't aware he was there to see it.

'No.'

At the other end of the phone there was silence.

'I will make sure nothing goes awry during filming. The next few days will be crucial for you. We will continue as we discussed.'

'Rashid—'

'We agreed.'

There was another lengthy pause. 'Bahiyaa shouldn't be alone. Should—'

'She is here.' Rashid motioned for his sister to come closer and passed her the receiver.

He turned his back to give her privacy, but he couldn't help but hear her side of the conversation. It was punctuated by long pauses in which he could only imagine what Hanif was saying.

'Perhaps it is better like this.' Another pause and then Bahiyaa said, 'Will you ring me as soon as you have... news?'

Quiet and dignified and completely in control of her emotions. Rashid heard the click as Bahiyaa ended the call and he came back to hold her in his arms.

She still didn't cry but stood so stiffly and he couldn't think of a single thing that might comfort her. Her father was dying, so angry with her he refused to see her. 'Do you want me to stay?' he asked softly.

'No.' Bahiyaa pulled back. 'Nothing has changed. I want Hanif to be Amrah's next king. Nothing must go wrong now. When he is King he will be able to give me my freedom.'

That was true. They had talked about it often. Bahiyaa clung to that with tenacity. It was her one hope.

'Omeir will never be able to touch me again. I can endure far more than being here alone knowing that.' She smiled. 'But I am sorry you have suffered because of me. You should be with our father.'

Rashid leant forward and kissed her cheek. 'I am sorry you are suffering because of his blindness. He is wrong and makes his own choice.'

'Where is he?' Baz asked, looking at his watch for the fifteenth time. 'This is ridiculous.'

'He's a prince, we are but mortals,' John quipped, pulling out a cigarette and patting his pocket for matches. 'Light, anyone?'

Polly said nothing. She watched the door, waiting for Rashid to reappear. To be called back like that couldn't be good. It had to be news about his father.

And she cared.

Polly shivered. What *was* happening inside?

Bizarrely, because the circumstances were so dissimilar, it brought back memories of her father's death. Details she hadn't thought of in years came flooding back. She remembered standing in Mrs Portman's red-carpeted hall listening while the other woman spoke about 'getting the little thing in her coat ready' and 'popping her in the taxi'.

Before then she'd thought her father would get better. That had been the longest drive of her life. Eight years old and she'd never been in a taxi on her own before. Her mother had met her at the hospital doors and had held her close.

Polly bit her lip so hard she drew blood. Rashid was no child of eight. Whatever was happening now he would be able to rationalise, but she ached for him. There was unfinished business between him and his father and that would haunt him for the rest of his life.

'Here he is! Now we can get going. 'Bout *bloody* time,' John said under his breath.

Polly spun round to look at Rashid, searching his handsome face for some sign of what had happened. There was nothing to see. His eyes were emotionless.

'I am sorry to have delayed you,' Rashid said by way of a greeting. 'Shall we leave?'

He barely spared her a glance. She shouldn't have expected he would, but it hurt that he didn't look to her. She felt so close to him. Connected.

Because she loved him.

The thought slid into her brain but it brought no surprise. *Of course*, she loved him. He'd let her see the man behind the prince. Nothing she'd read about him had prepared her for that.

She was in love with the man who shielded his sister. The man who loved his brother without rivalry. The man who had sat in the cool of the evening and listened to her. He was exciting. Compelling. A man she could trust with her life.

Except he didn't want that. She tempted him, but she was not what he wanted. He'd been conditioned to want an Arabian wife and she could never be that, however much she loved him.

Polly allowed herself to be steered into one of the waiting cars and, unlike last time, Rashid travelled alone.

She sat back in the soft leather seat, free to notice the way the convoy moved off in perfect unison and the way the outriders took their place at regulated intervals.

She knew what it was like to live among the British aristocracy, but this was a mode of travel she'd no experience of outside of Amrah. Despite the beauty of Rashid's palatial home she'd allowed herself to forget he was royalty.

She was in love with an Amrahi prince. A man of influence and power. No amount of physical chemistry was going to make anything other than a temporary relationship between them possible. It wasn't simply a matter of cultural divide. It was status, expectation, money, connections.

In backing away from their kiss Rashid had been kind. He'd not allowed her to hope.

'Where are we?' Pete asked, cupping his hand to peer out of the tinted window. 'Looks like we're heading for a private airport.' He whistled. 'There are helicopters waiting. Nice.'

All three cars came to a stop in perfect alignment. The motorcycle outriders dismounted and guards with guns took their positions.

'I suppose the great man didn't fancy driving.'

Or didn't think it was safe enough. That had to be a possibility, too. Rashid had personally guaranteed their safety. His father was dead or dying and he was here, keeping his word.

Polly hung back, watching as Rashid disappeared from sight and then waiting until she was directed which helicopter to go to. It was a couple of minutes, no more, before she was climbing in with the blades already spinning above. She settled herself in one of the seats, taking care to fasten the seat belt tightly across her lap, before looking up to see Rashid was at the controls.

It was a visual confirmation of the chasm between them. He lived a life of private planes, helicopters, race horses.

A prince.

She watched as he confidently ran through his pre-flight checks. Then, with a controlled lurch, the helicopter lifted up off the ground. Polly stared, glassy eyed, out of the window as Samaah became an aerial view, the modern motorways cutting a great swathe across it.

This was everything she had dreamed of seeing, the adventure she wanted, but she felt hollow inside. Around Samaah the countryside was vast and empty. For a time. Then the arid stony ground gave way to salt flats and, within minutes, she had her first glimpse of the Arabian Sea. Turquoise blue and edged with Amrah's famous white sands.

A town spread out in the shape of a pear drop and was dominated by three craggy forts, presumably built to protect from marauding forces from the sea. Al-Jalini. And as dramatically beautiful as anything she could have imagined.

Polly held her breath while Rashid swung the helicopter out over the sea and back towards town, coming to land on a designated helipad in the gardens of what looked like a fanciful sultan's palace. It was all arches, marble pillars and a stunning domed atrium.

Baz swore softly beside her. 'Like something out of *Ali Baba and the Forty Thieves*, isn't it?'

She nodded. It was exactly like that. A place for tourists who preferred their experience of Arabia to be sanitised. Polly released her seat belt and reached inside her bag for her sunglasses.

'Let's go.'

She nodded again and followed Baz and John as they stepped down from the helicopter into unexpectedly lush gardens. By the time she turned another pilot was at the controls and Rashid had come to stand beside her, tension radiating from him.

'What is this place?'

'The Al-Ruwi Palace Hotel,' Rashid answered her question crisply, his eyes focused on the helicopters hovering like gnats above. 'I'm sorry if the change of plan has unsettled you but it is safer to fly.'

Polly so desperately wanted to ask about his father. She wanted to reach out and smooth the crease between his eyebrows, kiss away the tiredness in his eyes. There was no opportunity, even had she dared. Baz joined them, smiling broadly. 'Fantastic view coming in. Just wished we'd had a chance to get some shots of that.'

'If you wish I can arrange it,' Rashid said, turning his attention to the second helicopter.

'Bikini-babes everywhere,' John whispered in her ear, reaching into his pocket for his packet of cigarettes. 'Bit different from Samaah.' He stepped away before lighting up and Baz wandered over to join him.

Polly took a sharp intake of breath. She couldn't wait any longer. She had to know. 'Was the news bad?'

A tell-tale muscle pulsed in his cheek. 'Expected.' Rashid met her gaze briefly. 'Hanif will ring when it is over.'

'Shouldn't you be there? With the rest of your family at least?' Rashid shouldn't be here babysitting a Western film crew he'd never really wanted to come.

'I have not been asked for.'

'And Bahiyaa?' She asked the question even though she knew the answer.

'Is content to remain in Samaah.'

'Couldn't she have come here with us?'

Rashid's face broke into a half-smile, the bleak look vanishing. 'To the desert? Bahiyaa would rather shave her head.'

Polly choked on a sudden laugh. It was strange how crying and laughter were so close. Flip sides of the same coin. 'She does hate it, doesn't she? She told me riding camels was a male preserve and that they were welcome to it.'

A frisson of awareness crackled between them.

'S-so, is that true?'

'Among the Bedouin people of the Atiq Desert, yes. Their womenfolk walk behind.'

'Sexist!'

His eyes smiled down at her. 'You have yet to sit on a camel. We will talk after.'

It was their only chance to talk before they were joined by her colleagues.

'I have taken the liberty of arranging rooms here at the Al-Ruwi Palace Hotel. Its security is tight and they're used to accommodating Western visitors. There are good sports facilities, a bar…'

'Did someone say bar?' John asked, looking about him for an ashtray only to have a uniformed hotel employee hurry over.

Polly soon wandered away. Down two broad steps to her right there were fifty or so chefs dotted along the edge of a sweeping circular courtyard and cooking on giant open grills.

'Who knew the Garden of Eden was in Amrah?' Pete said, coming alongside her. 'Something, isn't it?'

Polly looked at him curiously. This wasn't Eden. It was like some fabricated film set. Fun, but not real. Not at all like the beauty of the whitewashed and sand-coloured buildings they'd flown over.

'Rashid wants us to get our room keys and then we can explore what's available here.'

'Sorry. Yes, of course.'

The path meandered through improbable planting and passed four tennis courts. No one paid the slightest bit of attention to them until they walked into the exuberantly decorated reception hall. Then the Amrahi nationals noticed Rashid. Curious eyes turned on them from all directions and those nearest executed deep bows.

And Polly felt sad for him. Sad, not sorry. He wasn't a man you could feel pity for. But, sad, yes. Surrounded by people but essentially very alone. She hung back, noticing the care he took of other people. The skill with which he stopped them becoming over-familiar.

If she could she would have brushed them all aside and given him the peace and solitude he must want. Her own colleagues seemed oblivious to anything other than their own reasons for being in Amrah. It didn't even seem to have occurred to them that Rashid was greatly inconvenienced by their being there.

They didn't seem anything other than thrilled at the prospect of good sports facilities and a bar. Within minutes of noticing the sign they'd made plans for the rest of the morning, planning to meet as soon as they'd seen their luggage safely installed in their rooms.

'You don't like it here, do you?' Rashid said, making her jump.

Polly pushed her sunglasses back up on her head. 'It's…it's…er…' She glanced round at the flame colours of the opulent furnishings, the gilt decoration and mock-sultan palace touches. 'Do you?'

'It wasn't designed to impress for me.'

No, this was strictly for tourists. She glanced up at him.

'I suppose I've seen the real thing. It's not designed for someone like me either.'

Rashid's eyes warmed. 'Ah, but it has a licence to serve alcohol.'

'Naturally important,' Polly whispered back. 'Alcohol is always a primary consideration when you've chosen to holiday in a "dry" country.'

He laughed quietly, holding out a swipe card. 'You'll need this to get into your room.'

'Thank you.'

'And the lifts are this way,' Rashid said, pointing towards the left. 'I will show you the way to your room.'

Her smile wavered as she struggled not to let him see how aware she was of the fact they were alone. Her stomach felt as though it were a mass of frothy bubbles and the thoughts running through her head were a confusing muddle of contradictions.

She wanted to tell him his kiss was the most erotic thing she'd ever experienced—and, of course, she wanted him to know it hadn't bothered her at all. That she understood why he wouldn't want a relationship with her—and to scream at him that he was missing something wonderful.

Because it *would* be wonderful between them. The air was so completely charged when they were together. That couldn't just be one-sided. She didn't believe it. Breathing in, she caught the scent of his skin mingled with a manly fragrance and a shiver whipped through her as his arm brushed against hers.

She had never reacted to a man like this before. *She had never been in love before.*

A glass lift wafted them up to the fifth floor. Polly cleared her throat as the doors parted on a whisper. 'Are you on this floor, too?'

'Two floors above.'

More thoughts crowded into her head. She wanted him to know she understood completely that he'd want to be alone—but that he didn't have to be unless he wanted to. Sometimes, in the darkest times, you needed someone to sit with you, even though they were powerless to truly help.

Polly stepped out onto marble flooring. 'I think I'm that way,' she said, catching sight of the number 7.

'Yes.'

If he needed a friend she could be that. When she reached her room she stopped, checking the number on the door against the one on her swipe card. 'This is it.'

Did she ask him in now for a drink? Or did she offer to meet him for lunch? It *felt* different now they were in the hotel, as though Western rules applied. Not that that helped her much. It mattered too much to feel easy.

'Do you know how these things work?' she asked after her third try at opening her door.

His fingers brushed her hand as he took the swipe card and she swallowed hard.

'Like this,' he said, moving the card in front of a box, which flashed red. 'Now you can turn the handle.'

The door immediately swung open, a tantalising glimpse offered of the room beyond.

'I hope you will find the accommodation to your satisfaction.'

Polly closed her eyes and willed the words to leave her mouth. 'Would you rather be by yourself or would you prefer company?'

'Polly—'

'You must be thinking about your father. About Bahiyaa…'

She heard him exhale and steeled herself to turn round.

'It's going to be a long day if you spend it all by yourself.' She wished she had the right to walk into his arms and simply hold him. Hold him tight and make him feel loved, cared for and accepted. But she didn't. She could only talk. Take his mind off what he couldn't change.

Rashid's indecision was obvious. His firm jaw was clenched hard, his hands balled into fists by his side. Polly turned away and left him to follow or not.

She threw her handbag down on the king-size bed and fought an incongruous desire to laugh as she caught the full glory of the opulent crimson drapes tied back with oversized gold tassels. 'And you really ought to see this,' she said with the quickest of glances over her shoulder.

Rashid came in, the lines about his eyes deepening as he saw what she was pointing at.

'I thought the flame-coloured tea lights downstairs were tacky. But that's wonderful.' She moved over to investigate the room's tea and coffee facilities. 'Oh, and look, I can even do my own version of *gahwa*!'

He smiled but it was clearly an effort.

'I can be quiet, too,' she said gently.

He shook his head as though to deny he thought she needed to moderate her behaviour for him. 'Perhaps I ought to go? I am not very good company.'

'Sit out on the balcony for a while.'

He hesitated.

She peeked inside the mini-bar. 'I can offer you pineapple juice, orange juice, grape juice...with ice!' Polly said, holding up a small bag of ice cubes. 'Now, that's good.'

Again a smile that didn't quite reach his eyes. 'Pineapple with ice would be lovely.'

'This isn't going to compete with the fresh fruit juices you've given me,' she said, taking out two glass bottles.

'This looks exactly like the bottles we have at home.'
Polly placed a handful of ice cubes in the bottom of two
hi-ball glasses and poured the pineapple juice on top.

When she looked back Rashid had opened the French
windows. He didn't turn to smile as she came out to join
him. In fact, he didn't look at her at all. His eyes were
fixed on a distant point and he looked indescribably
weary.

Polly drew a quick shallow breath and then set the
drinks down on the table. He'd chosen to stay with her
rather than be alone.

'Is there a set time when your brother will call with
news?'

Slowly his eyes refocused on her. 'He will ring each
evening and, of course, earlier if there is anything to tell
me.' Rashid's fingers circled on the rim of his glass.

'And will he ring Bahiyaa or will you?'

'I think we will both call.' He paused, and then said,
'This is…kind of you.'

'This' being the drink, the sitting alongside him, the
being company. It felt as if someone had reached inside
her and were squeezing her heart so that it cried blood.

'I'm sorry you have to be here,' she said huskily.
'Babysitting us must be the last thing you want to be
doing.'

'It is needful.'

If they stayed with the revised itinerary he'd given to
them he'd have at least five days in this hotel. Two in the
Atiq Desert.

His father was dying. And he shouldn't be here.

Polly let the silence stretch between them. He would
talk if he wanted to and she wasn't about to force a conversation on him. What she really wanted to do was tell
him everything would be all right. But, of course, it wasn't

going to be. His father *was* going to die without Rashid having the comfort of a proper goodbye.

And she couldn't hold him. She shouldn't even reach out to hold his hand. The last time she'd done that it had snapped whatever semblance of control they'd had.

Rashid took a deep breath, seeming to make a conscious effort to rouse himself.

She smiled. 'I suppose the sooner we get this thing shot, the sooner you can go home. I'm not sure the guys are going to want to leave here and go home, though. Pete thinks he's stumbled into Eden and—'

Rashid leant across the table and captured her hand. His fingers interlaced with hers. Dark against the comparative paleness of her skin.

In such a short time she would be back at Shelton. Life would go on exactly as it had done for years. She would read about him, see photographs, but his life wouldn't touch hers again.

He might never hold her hand again. She had to remember this.

CHAPTER EIGHT

RASHID wasn't used to feeling so uncertain. He'd so much he needed to tell her—and the truth was he was reluctant to begin. Polly's beautiful blue eyes were shining with unshed tears. Tears he knew were there for him. Because she cared. He could count on the fingers of one hand the people who really cared about him.

And he was about to shatter her faith in him. If he was truly honest he was going to have to tell her about the suspicions he'd harboured about her. The decisions he'd taken because of that.

He was going to have to tell her that her home would be sold piecemeal. That he knew Shelton's famous Rembrandt was a copy, the original sold two years before. That it was quite possible the remaining Lovell family portraits, amassed over centuries, would be split up and sold to different collectors across the world.

That the detailed conservation programme she'd spent hours, weeks, months putting together would never be brought to fruition. That the young trees she'd had planted might never become the orchard she'd envisioned. That six years of her life had been devoted to something he'd decided to bring to an end.

Was it weak to want to delay the moment? His fingers moved against the palm of her hand. He was going to hurt her and Bahiyaa had known him better than he'd known himself. It was going to crucify him to do it.

'Wh-why are there *so* many copper coffee-pots here?' she asked, a break in her voice.

He loved it that she was nervous around him. Loved seeing the pulse beating at the base of her neck. All his adult life he'd been pursued by women. In the West it was almost entirely physical. Women who wanted the cachet of being known to be his lover. In Amrah, women wanted the status and security he could give them. Polly wanted neither, but her body betrayed her attraction to him and it excited him.

'The *dalla* is a symbol of Arabic hospitality,' he said, releasing her hand. 'The willingness to share what you have with others has its roots in survival.'

'Yes, but why *so* many? Even if this were a stage set you'd expect a few less. I love the idea of *gahwa*, though.' Polly took her sunglasses off her head, then slipped off the band she'd tied her hair back with. Rashid watched, distracted as she ran her fingers through the plait, loosening her hair into a curtain of waves that brushed her shoulders.

'Bahiyaa explained it. It's polite to drink two cups, so your host can feel bountiful, but not three, because that might expose him to want.'

He smiled.

'After you've drunk the second cup you shake it to show you've finished. Next time, if I manage to make it through the experience without fainting, I'll be ready.'

His eyes rested on her lightly sun-kissed face, her earnest expression, as she tried to keep talking so he would have something other than his father's illness to think about.

She was a woman who understood grief. She knew you needed to come in and out of it. In her company he found he could relax. He was interested in what she said and thought. He liked the way her eyes sparkled, the way they changed from blue to almost grey when she passed from happy to sad.

And he loved the way Polly wanted to explore a culture not her own. Her beautiful hands still showed the carefully drawn hennaed pattern his sister had applied, and would for days.

Her eyes followed his gaze. 'Bahiyaa painted it,' she said, self-consciously. Her forefinger traced the outline on her left hand. 'It took hours to dry. I don't think I've ever spent so long doing nothing in my entire life.' She looked up and smiled. 'I've enjoyed Bahiyaa's company so much. I will miss her.'

'And she you.'

'I wish I'd had a sister. Or brother. I think it would have been fun not to be quite so alone.' Then, 'Is…?' Polly stopped, biting the side of her lip.

'Go on.'

The tip of her tongue came out to moisten the very centre of her top lip. 'Is…?' She stopped again, then changed tack. 'Do you feel like an only child?'

Beautiful blue eyes looked across at him expecting an answer to a question no one had ever thought to ask him before. It took him to an area he'd suppressed because it had been easier to see his mother as 'bad' and to see himself only as his father's son.

But, of course, there were so many shades of grey— and the truth was his mother had been kind to her two stepchildren. Had loved them. The sibling bond he shared with Hanif and Bahiyaa had been forged then.

So, no, he didn't feel like an only child. Even though

his grandfather saw a distinction between Hanif and himself, they never had. They were brothers. Bahiyaa was their sister.

'Hanif was four when Princess Yasmeen died. Bahiyaa a baby. Neither of them have strong memories of their own mother.'

And they'd adopted his. They'd been a happy family. A unit. It was his father who had taken a mallet to it. It seemed so obvious now, but it came as a revelation.

'My mother was the only maternal figure they'd known.'

'So losing her was as difficult for them as you.'

No, that wasn't true. As painful and traumatic as his mother's leaving Amrah had been for them all, it was only he who had felt he had to rip out part of himself.

'Do they see her now?'

'Hanif has done.'

'And Bahiyaa?'

Rashid shook his head. 'She has never travelled outside of Amrah.'

'Never?' Polly's eyebrows shot up, her expressive face showing more than just amazement.

'She was married to Omeir at seventeen.'

Even as he said it the full force of what that had meant for Bahiyaa hit him. *Seventeen.* She'd endured a life sentence. Was still enduring it. It was perhaps just as well his father still refused to see him. Anger rolled over him. All the more potent because it had no outlet.

'Rashid.'

He looked up to see Polly watching him, her eyes concerned. Fearful.

'I could hate him,' he said, forcing the words out. There was no one else on earth he could say that to and know they'd hear it for what it was. 'I *do* hate him.'

'Don't.'

She reached out and took hold of his hand, as he had done hers. With infinite care she turned it over and smoothed her hand across his palm.

'My grandma believed the whole of your life was mapped out on the palm of your hand. Everything. Who you married. How many children. Whether you'd be sick. Prosperous.'

The light feather-soft touch of her fingers across his skin made it hard to concentrate, but his anger was evaporating like water in summer. She soothed him.

'She believed there was nothing we could do about any of it. But I've never believed there's a life mapped out for us. It has to be all about choices.'

Still those fingers moved over his hand.

'Some will be good and others not so good. You just have to hope you make enough good ones enough of the time to live a good life. Hating your father would be a bad choice.'

'What he's done is—'

'Wrong,' she finished for him. 'Your father is flawed. He made poor choices at some crucial points of his life. And those choices damaged other people. Hurt you. But he is dying, Rashid. You can be angry about some of the things he's done without forgetting the good things.'

And there *were* good things. It was that that ripped him in two. He wanted things to be black and white. Clearly right or wrong. A person good or bad. It was hard to admire his father so much, want his approval, and yet hate what he refused to put right for Bahiyaa. Then to realise he'd denied him a relationship with his mother and broken promises he must have made to her.

'Your time with him is running out. Can't you see your father before he dies?'

'Perhaps.'

But perhaps not. What had made his father such a good leader of men was his ability to make a decision and stick to it.

Polly's blue eyes were clear and strong. Without a doubt she would risk the rejection. He might, too, if it weren't for Bahiyaa.

'I will go if he asks for me. I cannot go without Bahiyaa.' Hanif aside, he had never spoken about this to anyone. Not even Bahiyaa, though he was sure she suspected.

'Four years ago,' he began, his voice scraping across razor blades, 'when Bahiyaa first came to me I went to see my father.'

It was painful to talk about, but with Polly it was possible. She radiated warmth. Acceptance.

'I told him. I told him about Bahiyaa.'

He had told him everything. He'd described her injuries in graphic detail: the bruises on her face and body, the broken bones and the mental scarring caused by years of living in fear. *Ten years*. He'd told him how Bahiyaa had suffered silently and struggled to cope.

'My father said that Bahiyaa had brought dishonour to our family and that he considered her dead to him. That as long as I chose to shelter her I was not welcome in his home.'

She frowned. 'You haven't seen him since Bahiyaa came to live with you four years ago?'

He nodded.

Polly sat back in her chair and looked at him. 'You are a remarkable man,' she said slowly.

Of all the things he'd expected her to say that hadn't been it. He couldn't have anticipated his reaction to her words either. It was like ice breaking deep inside him.

'I told you Bahiyaa was lucky to have you for a brother, but I hadn't realised quite how lucky. She must have been terrified.'

'She still is. And will be as long as Omeir continues to insist he wants her to come home.'

'Why does he want her to?' Polly reached forward to pick up her glass and drained the last of her pineapple juice.

Who knew? Any man who treated a woman as Omeir had treated Bahiyaa was someone beyond his comprehension. 'He says he loves her, but it's a warped kind of love. It may be pressure from his family. I don't know.'

'She can't go back.'

'No.' Bahiyaa would return to that life over his dead body.

'I should really mind my own business, particularly when it comes to things I don't know anything about. I hadn't realised what taking Bahiyaa in had meant for you. I just can't resist trying to sort everything and everyone out and sometimes they're just not fixable.'

She pulled her hair off her neck and, taking the band from her wrist, twisted it up into a loose ponytail. 'It's so hot. Do you want another drink?'

Rashid shook his head.

'I will.' She got up and went inside for a moment or two, returning with a second pineapple juice with twice the amount of ice. 'I'm sorry you can't see your father before he dies,' she said, sitting down again, 'but I think you're right. Bahiyaa needs you more. What does Prince Hanif say about it?'

'Very little. I've persuaded Hanif it's better if he doesn't. Bahiyaa is safe with me and that's really all that's important. There is nothing to be gained by both of us making the same sacrifice.'

'Difficult for him, though.'

'Yes.'

'I wish life wasn't so complicated,' she said on a sigh.

Rashid watched the shadow pass over her face, and wondered what she was thinking about, fearing he knew.

'It's *so* hot,' she said again, holding the iced glass against her cheek. 'How do people cope in summer?'

'By shutting the doors and giving thanks you live in an age of air-conditioning.' His head nodded towards the French doors propped open. 'It's an option now. You'd be cooler inside.'

She gave a soft laugh. 'That would feel like cheating. There was no air-conditioning when my great-great-grandmother lived here. I wonder how long it took her to adjust to the temperatures. You kind of imagine she'd have taken the whole thing in her stride, don't you?'

A shrill beep caught his attention. 'Is that your phone?'

Polly jumped up. 'Yes, I think it must be. I'm so rubbish with these things. Half the time I've not got it switched on and the other half I forget where I've put it.'

Rashid let his eyes wander out over the manicured gardens of the Al-Ruwi Palace Hotel while he waited for her to return. He still needed to tell her about her stepbrother. There was a situation that wasn't fixable.

'Well, that was Graham,' Polly said, returning. 'Just checking I didn't wish to join them for lunch. I'm really not that hungry when it's hot like this.'

'In Amrah we tend to opt for a simple rice dish midday,' he agreed, absent-mindedly. The trouble with delaying telling Polly the truth was that it felt dishonest, in a way it hadn't when he'd thought she might have been involved.

'Polly?'

She looked up.

'*Why* have you stayed at Shelton Castle? I know you love the house and that you grew up on the estate, but haven't you ever imagined something different for yourself?'

She looked up into his face, her eyes meeting and holding his.

That had to be the key to finding a way of ensuring Polly didn't suffer unduly. She had told him this was the first thing she'd ever done 'entirely for herself' and it was clear she was relishing everything about her Arabian adventure. She seemed to crave excitement. Yet she'd stayed with what she'd known from childhood. There had to be more to that decision than he knew—and if he knew why he would be in a far better position to offer her an alternative.

'What would you do if you had a completely free choice of what to do with your life?' he prompted.

'They're two very different questions.'

'And?'

'Why have I stayed?' she repeated slowly.

He nodded.

She hesitated, her eyes holding real sadness. 'I told you I initially came back because my mother was struggling to adjust to life as the Duchess of Missenden, didn't I?'

'Yes.'

'That…was true, but it was all a bit more complicated than that.' Her fingers splayed out on the table between them.

Rashid waited, by no means sure she would tell him anything.

She looked up. 'It concerns Anthony, so I need you to promise you won't tell anyone.'

She was lovely. The Duke of Missenden deserved no such loyalty and yet he had it.

'If any of this ended up in the British tabloids it would be horrendous.'

'I would never betray your confidence.'

'No. Sorry. It's just I never talk about the family.'

'*The* family' as opposed to '*my* family'. It was a distinction he was beginning to understand. Nick had been right in his assessment of Polly's role at Shelton.

'But it's hardly fair to ask you questions about yours and then refuse to tell you anything about mine. So…' She took a deep breath. 'In order to minimise death duties Richard had already passed ownership of the castle to Anthony by the time he married my mother.

'That's not unusual,' she said in response to his raised eyebrow. 'It really is the only way to make it possible for the great houses to be passed intact from one generation to the next. Crazy, isn't it? You'd think they could work out a better system but, anyway, that's what Richard did. It usually works well.'

But… Rashid waited for the 'but'.

Polly twisted one of her small stud earrings. 'Unfortunately for Shelton, Anthony is a gambler.'

She knew. Relief surged through him.

'Richard said he didn't know, but I think he must have. On some level, anyway. Everyone on the estate knew. But I think we thought Anthony wouldn't touch Shelton.'

'And he did?'

Polly nodded. 'Oh, yes, it's an addiction. As soon as Richard transferred ownership he borrowed huge sums against the house. Sold a number of small things he thought no one would notice.' She tried to smile, but it faltered almost immediately. 'My mother did, of course.'

Her blue eyes looked almost grey. Polly was miles away, thinking about a time that clearly gave her pain. Rashid could all too easily picture how difficult it must have been for the new Duchess to challenge her husband's heir on missing treasures.

'And there was nothing your stepfather could do?'

'He'd transferred ownership. Shelton was Anthony's. But, at the time, Richard and my mother were still living at the castle—' She broke off, drawing in a painful breath. 'Do you want to know all this? Really?'

'I want to know why you have stayed at Shelton.' If it hadn't been so important for him to know Rashid didn't think he could have forced her to continue.

She shrugged. 'Oh, well, this *is* the "why". I'd come home for the summer after I finished at uni. I had some vague plan about doing a PhD but, to be honest, I'd had enough studying for a bit and Richard asked me to help.'

Her face changed, softened, as kinder memories ran through her head.

'He was the loveliest man. Real old school. He believed he was the custodian of Shelton for future generations and his one aim had been to hand the castle on to his heir intact.'

'Only for the heir to start dismantling it.'

'Right. It began with some of the minor paintings Richard had put into storage. Pieces of china. A few clocks. They all went to pay the interest on the loans.'

'And your stepfather knew this?'

'By the time I came home he did. Anthony was quite scared, I think. Everything had snowballed so quickly and he agreed to let his father take on the day-to-day running of the castle again.'

The day-to-day running, which, having read that final report, he now knew was Polly's responsibility.

'We divided the jobs between us. My mother continued as housekeeper. Richard concentrated on the financial side of things. And I tried to drum up new money-making enterprises to make a start on repairing the roof.'

'Successfully?'

'To an extent. Shelton is a money pit. But it was interesting work and it seemed worth doing.' She looked to him as though she were searching for his approval. 'It was only meant to be a very temporary thing.'

Polly brushed a hand across her face. 'Richard was sure Anthony would seek help...'

And, of course, that hadn't happened.

'But, gambling is an addiction and the problem had been there a long time. Richard and my mother moved out of the castle into a house on the estate and that helped maintain the peace. Anthony and Georgina took up residence in the main house.'

'And you?'

'Moved back down to the staff quarters. Much nicer.' She took a breath before continuing, 'But then there was the accident.'

Rashid saw the pulse beat in her neck and her hands move convulsively against her glass. He asked gently, 'Is that how your mother came to be in a wheelchair?'

She swallowed hard, her voice husky. 'Three years ago in May they were coming back from a party. Richard was driving and he had a stroke. Their car hit a ditch and they somersaulted. My mother broke her back but Richard never knew. He had a second stroke within twenty-four hours and died.'

She brushed a hand across her eyes. '*Damn*, I'm sorry. I hate thinking of it.'

'So you stayed.'

'Of course. While I was waiting for her to come home I installed ramps in the ground floor of the house, lowered work surfaces, fitted a bathroom in part of the garage and made a bedroom out of the other part.'

Rashid didn't really need to hear the rest of her story. He could piece it together himself.

'The upstairs I turned into a flat for me and I moved out of the staff quarters. And I tried to take over the things my mother and stepfather had been doing.'

'Why?' He knew few women who'd put their life so comprehensibly on hold. Certainly not for the years Polly had. No wonder she craved adventure. Her life was boxed in by a combination of circumstance and misplaced loyalty.

'Minty says that. She says Shelton is Anthony's responsibility and that I need to move away.' Polly tried to smile. 'And I do. I know I do. Even my mother says I do. But it's hard to let Shelton go. Mentally I accept I need to, but I can't quite do it. It feels like I'm admitting failure.'

'It's not your failure.'

'But I know I'd be letting Richard down. I know he'd have wanted me to carry on as long as Anthony lets me. And, if I left, where would I go? My mother needs care. I have a strange CV.' She took another sip of her drink. 'I've got no references. Unless Anthony can be persuaded to write me one. And, even then, who'd believe it? He's my stepbrother. I'm not sure anyone would take that seriously.'

Rashid frowned slightly. 'Does Anthony *want* you to stay?'

'Hell, no. He'd like to sell the castle. Only he can't quite bring himself to do it while I'm there. It's as though I remind him of his father and make him feel guilty.'

As well he might. Rashid sat back in his chair. Richard had been a man not unlike his friend. From the moment he'd become the Duke of Aylesbury, Nick had spent every thinking, breathing moment planning the future of his crumbling pile of ducal stones. Absolutely determined to secure it for the son he hoped he'd have one day.

'And the Beaufort Stud?' he asked, drumming his fingers on the table. It was beginning to sound as though the only person he'd hurt by dismantling Shelton was Polly.

'It's owned by the Lovell family, and has been for three generations, but it's really Georgina's baby now. She's Anthony's wife, the present Duchess of Missenden.'

'Do you like her?'

'I don't know her. She considers me "staff".'

It was an unholy mess. 'Perhaps,' he suggested carefully, 'it would be better if your stepbrother sold the castle. Then its care could be entrusted to someone who would cherish it.'

'That won't happen.' Polly looked at him. 'Anthony will make much more money if he sells it off in bits and pieces. And I suspect the castle will be divided up into upmarket apartments, sold off on some kind of long lease. That would probably be enough to salvage his pride.'

Of course, she was right.

Most disturbing from his perspective was that, instead of taking from Anthony Lovell something he valued, he was allowing a weak man to abdicate responsibility for wasting his inheritance.

It needed thinking about.

'And my second question?'

Polly looked at him, bemused for a moment, then her eyes seemed to smile. He had no idea how they did that. They seemed to light up from within.

'What would I like to do?' She leant forward and thought for a moment or two, her elbows resting on the table. 'I don't know. I like being here. I like this.'

This. He liked this, too.

Being with her. Talking to her. Even though it wasn't comfortable listening.

'In the end I'll have to go home, though. My mother will always need care.'

'Do you own the house you live in?'

'My mother does.'

That was better than it could have been. At least Anthony couldn't sell it from under them.

'So you see I don't have very much time for dreams. I mustn't waste a moment.' Polly glanced down at her wristwatch. 'There are still over four hours before I need to meet the others.'

'Do you wish to rest?'

'No.' She looked slightly hesitant. 'I was wondering whether we might go and see something of Al-Jalini? Or do you need some time alone? I can easily explore the hotel complex.'

That was the last thing he wanted. Alone he'd have too much time to think. Rashid shook his head. 'It will be a pleasure to show you something of my country.'

An opportunity to salve his own conscience, too. He was as guilty as anyone of not considering Polly's wishes. He might have more justification than most, but he'd arbitrarily taken decisions that would affect her profoundly. 'Where do you wish to go?'

'I don't mind. Somewhere that isn't on the itinerary, perhaps?' she suggested, her eyes sparkling.

Adventure. She craved adventure. And the real Arabia.

'I will arrange that,' he said, standing up. 'There is somewhere I should like to show you.' He smiled. 'Somewhere I think you will like.'

CHAPTER NINE

POLLY let Rashid go. She shouldn't have asked to leave the hotel. Her smile became rueful as she gathered up the glasses and carried them through to her bedroom. She'd a pretty good understanding now of what forces were at work in Amrah. The timing of their visit was difficult. And she ought to be co-operating with the plans Rashid had already put in place, not making things more complicated.

But maybe it would be good for him, too. The cold, shut-down look he'd worn earlier had vanished while they'd been talking.

Polly walked over to the dressing table, her own brush and comb laid out. Her make-up bag to one side. She turned her head to look at her suitcase resting on a stand.

Everything must have been unpacked. She didn't even bother to check. It didn't seem to matter if some faceless someone thought she ought to buy better quality underwear. She had other things to think about. Problems that would all be waiting for her when she got home.

She sat on the edge of the king-size bed and searched her handbag for the small folded piece of paper on which she'd written the international dialling code for the UK and the number of the Al-Ruwi Palace Hotel. Phoning home felt difficult. Her mum refused to talk about what was happening at the castle, saying she preferred to hear all about her daughter's travels, but Polly knew her too well. She could hear the weariness in her voice, the false brightness.

Today was no exception. Her mother was pleased to hear from her. Keen to tell her that Mrs Ripley, who came each morning and evening to help her get in and out of bed, was wonderful. That she'd been out to dinner with friends, and insisted they could talk about the quotes that had arrived from three local plumbers when Polly got home.

Polly ended the call absolutely certain all was not well. Anthony had become more acerbic of late and it was usually her mother he took his frustrations out on. Without her there to deflect the snide comments Polly imagined she'd be having an unpleasant time of it.

And it made her feel more trapped than ever. How could she ever leave? It wasn't in her nature to walk away from people who needed her, but coming to Amrah had made her realise she did want more.

The soft tap on her door startled her, but it brought her head up. She was not going to spoil the now. Time with Rashid was precious, because whatever the future did hold for her it certainly did not hold Amrah's playboy sheikh.

Fixing a smile, she opened the door, but it couldn't have been very convincing because Rashid immediately asked, 'Are you feeling well?'

Polly brushed a hand over her eyes. 'I'm fine. I've just rung home.'

'Are there problems?'

'My mother assures me everything is "wonderful", but I don't believe her.'

'Polly,' Rashid said, stepping close. The lines around his mouth were more defined than she had ever seen them. 'Polly, if there is anything you are worried about, at Shelton, please talk to me.'

She laughed, the sound breaking on a hiccup. She believed Rashid was a man who could move mountains, but the problems at Shelton Castle were beyond his fixing. 'I think you've got enough going on in your life without me pouring out the nonsense in mine.'

Polly turned away to search the drawers for the blue *lihaf* Bahiyaa had insisted she pack.

'Polly—'

She found the scarf and pulled it out. 'I ought to take this. It's so hot out there.'

Rashid nodded, his expression unutterably weary. *His beautiful, strong face.* Polly felt a sharp pull on her emotions, an intense compulsion to smooth the worry lines from his forehead, to reach out and cradle his face between her hands and kiss away everything that was bothering him.

He must be under so much pressure from all sides. It put her troubles into perspective. The future of a kingdom was surely more important than that of a house, however beautiful.

'Are you sure you want to do this?' she said.

'Of course.'

'Really?'

'I would like to spend time with you.'

If she hadn't fallen for him before, she'd have fallen then. Rashid held out his hand and Polly put her own in it, trying to ignore the sense of nervous anticipation.

'Where are we going?'

'You will see.'

The curl of excitement in her abdomen spread. 'Are we walking?'

Rashid smiled down at her, his eyes softening. 'You will see.'

He wasn't going to tell her, but it didn't matter where she was going. She was collecting memories, storing them up against a future that was going to be without him. Rashid led the way back to the glass lifts and, before the doors opened, released her hand, resting his in the small of her back, guiding her in.

She was a twenty-first-century woman, used to holding her own doors open, but that tiny gesture made her feel protected and cared for. Polly glanced surreptitiously up at the darkly handsome man beside her, his skin tawny gold and his chin firm. Tall, broad-shouldered and powerful. She was no size zero but he managed to make her feel delicate. And the expression in his eyes when he looked at her made her feel desirable.

It had been a long, *long* time since she'd felt that.

Rashid didn't touch her again, but she could feel the energy pulse between them. Intense, scary and completely wonderful. She wanted him with a passion that surprised her. One that made a mockery of her morality.

She'd never been promiscuous. Far too much of a people watcher to ever want to be. She'd never understood women who slept with men who clearly viewed their relationships as recreation.

Men like Rashid. He might not be prepared to accept an arranged marriage, but when the time came she was sure he wouldn't choose any of the women he'd been linked to in the British press.

But she was tempted. More than tempted. Would it be wrong? Loving him, would she survive the inevitable parting?

The lift doors slid open and Polly held back as a man stepped forward and bowed. 'All is ready, Your Highness.'

Rashid spoke in Arabic. Then turned back to her. 'The helicopter is waiting for us.'

'We're going by helicopter?'

'Yes, of course.'

Of course. In his world it was just another form of transport. He was an Amrahi prince. He lived in a palace. And for today, right now, he was hers. She wasn't going to think outside this moment.

Where were they going?

'I've only got a few hours before I've got to meet the boys in the foyer.'

'You will not be late.'

'Rashid—?'

He laughed softly. 'Patience.'

For a while she said nothing more, content to be with him. She watched as he went through the pre-flight checks, loving the strength of his hands on the controls.

'Just us?' she asked in surprise as the last of his staff prepared to leave them.

Rashid looked at her. 'We will be safe enough where we are going. Are you scared?'

Not about going without security, no. Of how she reacted to him, yes. She didn't quite recognise the woman she was when she was near him. It *was* frightening, but exciting, too.

'There is no need.'

'I suppose not,' she managed. 'We're not going to be where anyone expects us to be. That has to be safer than following a planned itinerary.'

He smiled and Polly settled back in her seat. This was a golden day. A day that would live on in her head always as being pure magic.

And she still had absolutely no idea where he was taking her. She managed a few minutes, but then she couldn't resist asking again.

'You are a hard woman to surprise,' Rashid said as he took the helicopter along the line of the coast.

Polly turned her head away from him to hide her smile. 'I'm not really used to it.'

Below her the harmonious blend of Al-Jalini's sand-stone buildings gave way to a bizarre collection of… houses. Were they houses? She peered closer. 'What are the buildings with the brightly coloured plastic roofs? There.'

Rashid barely needed to glance below him. 'Homes. Traditionally they'd have been thatched, but people improvise with what they have.'

Plastic?

'The walls are made with interlocking sticks. Farther inland it tends be flattened-out oil drums. Over the border into Oman there are *barasti*, which are homes built from palm leaves. It's what's easily available and will provide shelter at little or no cost.'

She hadn't seen that in Amrah before. Samaah was a vibrant and affluent city, Rashid's palace pure fantasy. This was grinding poverty.

'Change takes time,' Rashid said, his eyes on her profile. 'And people are resistant to change. My father insisted affordable housing was built on the outskirts of Al-Jalini, and there are jobs here, but many have preferred to remain in their own communities.' Rashid took the helicopter sharply inland.

'How much farther?'

She caught the edge of his smile. He didn't answer, concentrating on bringing the helicopter down on a flat plain near a dusty hillside.

'Here?' Polly sat up straight in her seat, looking out of the window in disbelief.

He laughed.

'There's nothing here.'

'Look closer.'

She did, and looked out at a collection of puny trees clinging to an arid dusty hillside. A desolate, bleak place.

'As far back as five thousand BC this area was an important centre for frankincense.'

'What happened? Is this climate change?'

Rashid laughed again, jumping down from the helicopter and walking round to help her. He reached up and Polly put her hand in his. She looked down at him and her smile faded as the air crackled between them.

'Jump.' The rich timbre of his voice seemed to reverberate in her chest. His eyes, and the sensuality in them, sent heat to every extremity of her body.

Being with him felt like that. Like jumping. Not sure how safe the landing would be, but knowing the experience would be worth it. If she dared.

'Come.'

Polly lowered herself down, steadied by Rashid's grip on her hand until her feet touched the ground and she became aware of his left hand resting low on her waist. He was so close. She could feel the strong, hard planes of his torso. Even feel the beat of his heart.

Neither moved. A handful of centimetres apart and the moment stretched on. And on. Polly waited, her eyes caught by the fierce intensity of his.

She dragged air into lungs that had seemed to forget they had a function as his hand moved to cradle her cheek, his palm warm against her face. His eyes impossibly tender. He moved so slowly. There was time, plenty of time to pull back if she'd wished to, but she didn't.

She stood there waiting to breathe.

This kiss was different. Different from before. This time she knew she loved him and that changed things.

Polly closed her eyes, savouring his breath on her lips before the first fleeting touch of his mouth.

So teasing. Warmly sensual.

His touch was almost reverent.

Polly felt the fear recede. She wanted this. For however long, whatever he could give her.

She wanted him to remember this moment.

Remember her.

Her lips parted and Rashid's hold on her head became firmer, his kiss more insistent.

Warm. Soft. Sexy. She felt as though she were melting from the inside out, and that had nothing to do with the strong Amrahi sun.

His tongue traced the line of her bottom lip and her hands clung to him as passion engulfed her. A tsunami-type wave that swept away everything before it. And, finally, she understood what had prompted Elizabeth to leave her family.

This. It was this.

The desire for this and its discovery. There was nothing clean and sanitised about this emotion. It was raw. Dangerous. Compelling.

Her fingers closed on the material of his *dishdasha*, the air warm and sultry around her and her senses full of the scent of his skin, of spice and musk.

Slowly, his eyes watching for her reaction, he pulled back. His right hand moved to pull the band from her hair, the silky softness falling about her face as Rashid reached for her again. His mouth compelling and sensual.

She loved him.

Loved him.

His tongue slipped into her mouth and she felt her tremble the length of her body, a fierce dragging sensation of need low in her stomach. His hands, either side of her face, held her prisoner.

'Polly.' Rashid's voice was hoarse, almost desperate. His arms held her close, his forehead resting on hers, waiting for the world to steady.

He eased back, one thumb tracing the line his tongue had taken over her sensitised bottom lip. 'You enflame me.'

And you me.

'I do not wish... I have no right to seduce you.'

Polly reached out and traced the deep indenture by the side of his mouth. 'I kissed you back,' she whispered.

'Polly, I...' The words seemed wrenched from him, his hold on her convulsive. 'Not now. This cannot happen.'

He was right, of course. He couldn't make love to her on a dry and dusty hillside, but the feeling of rejection was intense. She'd all but offered herself to him. And she'd never done anything like that before in her entire life.

This cannot happen.

She wanted to ask why. More than anything she wanted to change his mind. But Rashid had already stepped back.

'This afternoon was supposed to be for you. I wished...' He rubbed an impatient hand across his face. 'I want you to have memories to take away with you. Good memories.'

So did she. She wanted those memories filled with him.

'Polly, I—'

'Don't!' She didn't want to hear any explanations of anything. She was doing well to be still standing. If it had been possible she'd have taken herself away to a dark place and curled herself in the smallest possible ball. 'I understand.'

'Polly.'

'No, really. It's fine.' She neatly sidestepped him and

stood looking out at the desolate place he'd brought her to. 'Where does frankincense come from now?'

'Here.' Rashid moved closer. 'The fabled golden city Queen of Sheba saw has long gone, but the trees are still here.'

Polly blinked hard, fiercely determined to pretend she was just fine.

'All that has really changed is its commercial value. Frankincense is no longer as valuable as gold. Once upon a time men made their fortunes trading it against spices from India and caravans took it across the entire continent.'

He started towards the stony and uneven ground. Polly followed, still bemused as to how this bleak landscape could ever have been a golden city. Rashid stooped and picked up a sharp stone, which he then jabbed against the flaky tree bark.

Polly watched as an oozing blob of sap bubbled up out of the slash in the tree. 'That's frankincense?'

'And it's still harvested today and sold around the world.' He pulled a bit and rubbed it between his finger and thumb. It gathered together into a glutinous ball which he flicked away.

'I'd no idea it came from trees.'

'As a child I thought it was magical.' He seemed to be lost in thought, as though a bittersweet memory was crowding in around him.

His father was dying.

Immediately Polly felt guilty. There must be so much going on in his mind. Huge pressures crushing in on him. Nothing mattered so much in the face of that. She reached out and caught his hand. 'Thank you. For showing me this.'

Rashid looked down to where their fingers were

joined. His thumb moved against her palm. 'There is somewhere else.'

'Wh—?' she began, but he shook his head.

'You will see. Come, there is plenty of time yet.'

It would have been possible to negotiate the uneven ground alone, but she liked the feel of his hand in hers. 'Can you land these things anywhere?' she asked as they approached the helicopter.

Rashid lifted their joined hands and pressed a kiss against the inside of her wrist. 'That depends on the skill of the pilot.'

'Can *you* land them anywhere?'

His blue eyes took on a sinful glint. 'You had better hope so.'

Polly's stomach performed a complete somersault. She climbed up into the helicopter and settled herself into the seat. Was it really possible to fall in love so completely and so quickly? Or was this like a desert mirage, nothing more than a distant reflection?

She glanced over at his strong profile. She only knew she'd give up everything to be with him. If he asked her to. This place, this country… She could love it.

Within moments they were airborne, the frankincense trees dotted below her. 'Has anyone tried to find the city?'

'Archaeologists. Adventurers.' Rashid turned his head to look at her and smiled. 'Your great-great-grandmother. No one has yet found incontrovertible proof one way or the other. Amrah is a country which holds its secrets closely.'

A mystical land. Polly stared out of the window as the stony land gave way to scrubby sand and, in the distance, wide-open desert. She turned back to Rashid. 'The Atiq Desert?'

He nodded and excitement whipped through her body.

'Not where you plan to film, but my home. The place I return to.'

The Atiq Desert stretched out endlessly. Not as she'd imagined it. It was a landscape studded with volcanic remains. Jet-black against the pale gold of the sand.

'It's amazing.' Then, 'There are people.'

'Bedouin. "Conquerors come and go, but it is only the Bedouin who stay,"' Rashid quoted softly.

'Camels! Rashid…'

Rashid wished he could watch her face, but he needed to concentrate on landing safely. Her excitement was contagious. Whether or not the reality of Bedouin life would live up to her romantic dreams he couldn't say, but he wanted her to experience it.

In many ways, if it didn't it would help when the time came to watch her leave. And she would leave. She'd return to a life he was dismantling. Khalid would already have acted on his instructions. He'd wondered, today back at the hotel, whether her mother had said something and that was why she'd been crying.

She had been crying. And he'd ached for her. For what he was about to do to a place she loved so much. If she knew would she still quiver in his arms? Bahiyaa's words echoed in his head: 'I do not think she will be able to forgive you that, Rashid.'

'Have they come to meet us?' Polly asked, turning back from the stationary cameleers and their bad-tempered charges.

Rashid landed the helicopter with minimum sand disturbance. 'You wished to ride a camel.' He smiled at her inarticulate squeal beside him.

'You arranged this. How? But, how did you do this in such a short time?'

'I am a prince,' he teased, 'and we princes of the

desert have a centuries-old method of communicating with our own.'

Polly wasn't fooled for a minute. Her eyes sparkled. 'You used a mobile.'

'Even the Bedouin have cell phones these days,' he agreed.

She was addictive, Rashid thought, loving the low chuckle she gave. If he could he would do more than this for her. Any dream she had he would strive to give her.

Anything that did not touch on his honour.

Anything but Shelton's reprieve.

'This is incredible! And Elizabeth came here?'

'With King Mahmoud. Without a doubt. This is his tribe. His people.'

'Am I dressed all right?' Polly asked suddenly, reaching down for her *lihaf*.

'You are beautiful. And you are with me. These men are my friends, my kin.'

Her beautiful eyes looked up at him.

'And,' he said with a smile, 'they will think you are dressed very unwisely.'

Polly smiled and twisted the scarf around her head, the blue of the *lihaf* bringing out the deep sapphire colour of her eyes. She was more than beautiful. And he felt a fierce spurt of pride at the thought these men would think she was his.

His.

A possessive word. A word that sounded good to him.

Kareem, the man who had first sat him on a camel, came forward to greet them, bowing low.

Rashid moved close to Polly, saying quietly, 'They do not speak any English.'

There was no time for any more before the *chanteur* offered his welcome. *'Ahlan beekum. As-salaam alaykum.'*

'*Wa alaykum as-salaam,*' Polly replied formally. She shot a mischievous look in his direction. 'How was that?'

Her pronunciation needed a little work but it was impressive. As she was a foreigner, an *ajnabi*, not one of the men present would have expected that. He hadn't. But Polly was a continual surprise to him.

Rashid went through the important process of enquiring after everyone's health, one eye on Polly as she took in the camel asserting his male dominance by blowing out his throat lining.

Her blue eyes looked to him for reassurance and he smiled. 'Ready?'

'For what?'

'Your camel ride?'

Polly looked hesitantly at the wizened little man coming towards her, gesturing back at a large one-humped camel. That had been her fantasy, but faced with the reality she was less sure. It was really only the glinting amusement in Rashid's eyes that spurred her on.

She pointed at the camel, hoping her body language would convey what needed to be said.

Kareem nodded, stopping by a white camel. 'Ashid.'

'*Ashid?*' Polly queried, looking back at Rashid.

'The name of your camel,' he said, strolling over with a smile.

Polly was pleased Ashid hadn't been the one blowing out its neck like bubblegum. She turned, disconcerted, when Kareem started to make a noise that she could best describe as being like a cappuccino machine.

'He's asking it to sit.'

After a moment's hesitation Ashid obliged, sinking down on its knees. Perilously perched on top of the single hump was a roll of fabric.

This couldn't be any harder than mounting a horse,

Polly told herself firmly. She allowed Rashid to help her sit astride. 'Tuck your feet up behind,' he instructed, 'and grip with your knees.'

He'd barely finished speaking before Kareem gave an instruction that had Ashid lurching upwards. Polly let out a shriek and looked down to see Rashid's laughing eyes watching her. She clutched at the makeshift saddle, glad another one of the cameleers had Ashid firmly on a lead.

She was too busy trying to get her feet up behind her to watch Rashid climb on his own 'ship of the desert'. The heat was sizzling hot, scorching through the light scarf. Polly looked curiously at the turbanlike headgear the Bedouin wore, but Rashid was too far away to ask anything about it and within moments she was concentrating on adjusting to the camel's movement.

Once she'd got used to the bouncing it was reasonably comfortable. The heat was something else. Minty's insistence they try to film everything during the cooler months made absolute sense. Polly kept her eyes firmly on the tree they seemed to be making for.

It had the appeal of lights flickering in a cottage window on a stormy night back home. It spoke of safety and rest. But she loved every minute of her camel ride. She turned round to smile at Rashid, so happy she wanted to laugh.

Her desert prince looked as though he'd been born to ride a camel. Which, in a way, he had. The animal's uneasy gait didn't produce the same lurching it did for her. He was able to talk to the men walking beside him, laughing as one of them struck up a tuneless chanting. From the other men's reactions she assumed the lyrics were probably quite rude.

'So was Bahiyaa right? Do you think riding camels should be reserved for men?' Rashid asked as she inelegantly climbed off Ashid.

'I think the jury is still out.' Her legs felt a little as if they'd turned to jelly. Rashid seemed aware of that because he reached out to steady her, his hand coming to rest on the small of her back.

'You did well.'

She laughed. 'Surprised?'

'Not as much as I thought I'd be,' he answered. 'Now we get lunch and a rest before we head back to Al-Jalini.'

Polly walked gratefully under the shade of the shrubby tree. 'Is this an acacia tree?'

He nodded, pulling the rolled fabric off Ashid and bringing it over for her to sit on.

'How does it survive out here?'

Rashid came to sit beside her. 'It has root systems which spread out a hundred feet or more. As you get nearer the wadi there are considerably more than here.'

She watched as the cameleers tied the front legs of the camels together, turning to Rashid with an impulsive, 'Does that hurt them?'

'No. Annoys them, perhaps,' he said. 'There is a saying among the Bedouin that you should never trust a camel. You can't take any chances. To lose your camel out here would be like being shipwrecked.'

Polly had thought she'd read fairly extensively, but there was so much she wanted to know. Everything about the Atiq Desert fascinated her. The men had already lit some kind of a brazier. Kareem was involved in a complicated process of pouring liquid from one pot to another from a flamboyant height.

'Wh—?' she began.

Rashid settled back into the shade of the tree, more at peace than Polly had ever seen him. He'd described this as his home, and it seemed it was. His palace home was sumptuous, but it came with much responsibility.

Here there was just space. Quiet, all bar the sound of camels complaining and munching on the thorny branches of the acacia tree. It felt so much like sitting in the centre of history. The birth place of three world religions. The petty squabbles of Shelton, her concern over its long-term future, suddenly seemed so very unimportant.

She turned her head to find Rashid was watching her, his blue eyes unfathomable. 'This is the most amazing place I've ever seen.'

He smiled.

'What is he doing?' she asked with a look at Kareem.

'Making tea.'

She looked back as the cameleer poured the liquid into several glasses already laid out on a tray.

'Water is precious here and is treated like vintage wine.'

Polly knew Rashid's eyes didn't leave her face as she first sipped the frothy tea. Over the rim of his own glass, Rashid's eyes were wickedly teasing.

'*Shukran,*' she murmured as Kareem returned her glass a second time. The flavour was slightly different. Sweeter. Perhaps a result of tea and sugar continuing to blend.

In twenty-seven years Polly didn't think she'd ever experienced such peace. It was partly Rashid, partly the incredible privilege of being here in a magical place he loved. Real happiness bubbled inside her.

The tallest man, the one who'd guided Ashid, stretched out some dough rather as you would a pizza. It was all fairly surreal. As meals went it was one of the simplest she'd ever eaten. She'd no idea what the men around her were saying, but she loved the laughter and their easy camaraderie.

'It's time we were leaving,' Rashid said, breaking in on her thoughts.

Polly experienced a wave of disappointment and then her innate sense of responsibility kicked in. 'I wish… I hope I can come back here one day.' She smiled up at him, fighting an inexplicable desire to cry. 'Thank you.'

Rashid caught her chin, tilting her face so that he could look deep into her eyes. 'Pollyanna Anderson, you are a re-markable woman,' he said, almost echoing her words to him.

It wasn't a declaration of love, not in any conventional sense, but it felt like it.

CHAPTER TEN

THE flight back to the Al-Ruwi Palace Hotel seemed to take no time at all. Al-Jalini, beautiful though it was, didn't have the charm of the desert and the hotel gardens were an unnatural splash of green.

Polly felt as if she'd left a little piece of her heart behind. She looked down at her watch. 'I should have time for a shower before I meet the boys,' she said with false brightness. 'Then we're off to the souk. According to Dr Wriggley it's one of the oldest in Amrah.'

Rashid nodded. 'You'll walk under the same tall arch Elizabeth did.'

'Will you be there?'

Polly saw the muscle pulse in his cheek and knew his answer before he gave it. 'There is no need. You will have security with you.'

She could feel him slipping away from her. 'What will you do?'

'Work.' His monosyllabic reply set her at a distance. She knew, logically, that he would have to. He'd taken hours off today to help the film crew, ensuring their safety, and then spending time with her this afternoon. But…

It felt more than that. As though the weight of the world had come back to rest on his shoulders.

'When will you speak to Prince Hanif again?'

'This evening.' Rashid brought the helicopter down on the hotel's helipad. Within seconds her door was opened and hotel staff were helping her down.

Polly flicked the scarf from her head and shook out her hair as Graham ambled over. 'Where have you been?'

She felt a ridiculous reluctance to tell him. It was as though the sound man was trying to force his way into something intensely precious. Private. 'We've flown over the Atiq Desert,' she evaded, turning back to watch Rashid step down from the helicopter.

He came over. 'I will leave you.'

There was nothing Polly could say. Not with Graham overhearing every word. And that was probably just as well, because what was there to say? She wanted to reach out and touch him. Hold him. Take the pain of whatever he was experiencing away, make it hers.

Rashid held himself stiffly, completely inaccessible. The man she'd kissed so passionately had vanished.

'Graham.' He nodded at the other man. 'I will see you both later this evening, perhaps?'

By the time Steve had decided they'd filmed enough for the day Polly was exhausted. She'd walked up and down one section of the souk more times than she could remember, each time exclaiming at the same stalls of silverware. She'd loved the canopied roof of palm fronds, the feeling of walking in the footsteps of her great-great-grandmother, but her mind had been elsewhere.

It was with Rashid, wondering whether he'd any news about his father. Whether he'd spoken to Bahiyaa.

'Drink?' John asked as they walked into the foyer. 'Or shall we get something to eat first?'

'What about the prince? Might be a good idea to ring up? See if he wants to join us?' Baz looked over at the reception area and then back at them. 'What d'you reckon?'

'Do it,' John said. 'We'll wait in the bar. Come find us.'

Polly let herself be guided towards the largest of the hotel's bars, edged with small seating booths. She missed the quiet of the desert. She wanted to be with Rashid. There was a slight possibility he might decide to join them, but she doubted it.

She sat cradling her chilled pineapple juice, one eye on the entrance watching for Baz to return. The tall Yorkshireman walked over shaking his head. 'Nope. Didn't actually get to speak to Sheikh Rashid. Spoke to his aide. The one from Samaah. He flew in an hour or so ago,' he said, pulling a face. 'I think the Crown Prince might be a goner.'

Polly put her pineapple juice down on the table. 'Did he say that?'

'No. Didn't say anything at all which is why I think there's been some bad news. Wasn't supposed to be here, was he?'

Pete pushed a beer across in Baz's direction. 'What'll that mean to us?'

'We'll be out of here, won't we? No way Minty is going to keep us here if it looks like the country is going to be unstable for a bit.'

There were a few disgruntled murmurs.

Baz added, 'She didn't like the changes to the itinerary. Think she'd have had us home then if she hadn't wanted not to offend Sheikh Rashid. I reckon we'll be out.'

Polly quietly slipped away, leaving her juice scarcely

touched on the table. Baz was almost certainly right in thinking Karim Al Rahhbi's arrival at the hotel couldn't be a good sign. She wasn't quite sure what she actually intended to do now. She simply knew she couldn't sit there making small talk when Rashid might need her.

She'd no particular reason for thinking it, but she suspected he'd told her things about his family he'd not discussed with anyone else. Other people might know that when Prince Khalid died Rashid would lose the father he loved and any hope of reconciliation with him, but she knew how he truly felt about that. He hadn't had a chance to say 'goodbye'. Nothing that would make the loss of his father easier to bear.

Polly hesitated at the main reception desk and then turned towards the glass lifts. Vaguely she remembered the guys talking about Rashid being booked into the penthouse suite. That seemed likely and it was quite possible they wouldn't give that information out at the desk even if she asked them. Better to go and see.

It wasn't until the lift doors opened on the seventh floor she wondered what she was going to actually *do*. She'd been acting on pure instinct, but now she realised it might be a little more complicated than to burst into his suite and demand to see him.

She was such an idiot. Karim Al Rahhbi would be there. Security staff. He wouldn't be alone.

But he still might need her.

Polly wrenched her bag open and pulled out the piece of paper on which she'd written the numbers she'd needed when she called her mother. It was the best idea she had. Better anyway than being turned away at the door.

She rang the hotel's number and waited while the receptionist answered. 'Hello, I'm Ms Pollyanna Anderson from Room 7 on the fifth floor. Can you put me through to His Highness, Prince Rashid bin Khalid bin Abdullah Al Baha's suite please?' She even managed to sound confident.

Even so, she was slightly surprised when the line crackled and a voice spoke. 'Miss Anderson, this is Karim Al Rahhbi. The prince is resting—'

'Yes, I know.' She cut across him. 'Ask him if he wants to speak to me.'

There was a significant pause while Karim decided to do just that. 'I will do so,' he said in his perfectly correct English. 'One moment, Miss Anderson.'

The line crackled again and it seemed to Polly it stayed that way for the longest time. More than enough time to realise what a huge assumption she'd made. The last thing she wanted to do was to make things more difficult for Rashid—and she didn't want to embarrass herself either.

The truth was *she* had a need to be here because she loved him. She couldn't bear knowing he was hurting and not be with him. That didn't mean he felt the same way.

And then came the realisation Rashid's aide might have flown to Al-Jalini on entirely different business. Rashid might have declined joining them because he preferred other company. He might…

'Polly?'

The pressure in her heart on hearing his voice was painful. 'Is there news? We thought—'

'My father has died.'

'Oh, Rashid. I'm so…*so* sorry.'

It was the end, then. Of so many things.

Polly stood clutching her mobile phone, so many thoughts passing through her mind. She thought of Bahiyaa. Of Rashid. Of what it would mean to Amrah.

And she thought of Minty and knew she'd be flying back to the UK first thing in the morning.

It was possible they'd return to Amrah to finish making their programme, but that would only be if there was political stability. There would be no need for her to see Rashid after today. Their lives would separate, just as she had always known they would.

She might see him again at a distance. At Shelton, perhaps, surrounded by beautiful women vying for his attention. As they'd been that first time. Or perhaps she'd never be any closer to him than seeing a picture in a magazine.

'Where are you?'

It was tempting to lie. 'I'm outside.'

'Outside?'

'Your suite,' she clarified. 'Seventh floor. Just by the lifts.' Nothing quite like committing emotional suicide, Polly thought. If he hadn't realised she'd fallen in love with him he'd surely know it now. Her heart was beating so hard it actually hurt.

And then she saw him, standing at the far end of the corridor, phone to his ear.

'Polly.'

'Hello.' She pulled the phone from her ear and ended the call. 'I wanted to know what had happened. Was it peaceful? The end?'

Rashid held his phone loosely in his left hand. 'I believe so. I scarcely know, I…'

He brushed his free hand across his eyes. 'Come in.'

She paused only long enough to stow her phone away in her bag, then walked slowly up the length of the corridor. What she wanted to do was run at him, wrap her arms around him and hold him so tight.

Reality wasn't quite like that, though. There was this enormous fear of being rejected, of having not quite understood what had been going on between them. And then there was Rashid's expression. The skin on his face appeared so pale it was almost translucent and his eyes were bleak. Unseeing.

He drew her in, past the bodyguards standing at the doorway. Karim stood up and moved to greet her. *'As-salaam alaykum.'*

'Wa alaykum as-salaam,' she murmured.

The one thing she didn't feel was 'peace'. Karim looked past her.

'Please leave us for a few minutes,' Rashid said. 'I will send for you the moment Miss Anderson leaves.'

What was left of hope shrivelled. She would be leaving. Soon. And Rashid had things he needed to be doing. Things that didn't involve her.

The door clicked shut. So quiet and yet it sounded loud to Polly. 'Have I broken some rule by coming here?' she asked, meeting his eyes properly for the first time.

Rashid shook his head. 'Karim is aware I have something to tell you. It must be done before you leave.'

'Am I leaving?'

Something flared in his eyes. For a moment Polly was glad to see an expression of something and then fear kicked in. She was leaving. He had said so.

'Within the next couple of hours,' Rashid concurred. 'Karim has already made all the necessary arrangements.'

Polly found herself a chair and sat down. That probably broke some Amrahi etiquette, but she wasn't so sure her legs were going to hold out much longer if she kept on standing. Everything was going wrong. It was happening and she was powerless to stop it.

'I have spoken to your friend, Miss Woodville-Brown, and she sees no reason to delay your departure.'

'Is there danger?' Polly asked in a small voice.

'There is a significant risk of terrorist incident.'

'I—'

'The choice isn't yours to make,' Rashid cut across her.

'No.'

'My grandfather is in shock and has yet to name his successor. He has three days.' Rashid paced across to the window and drew back the curtains.

From where she was sitting Polly could see the garden illuminations, Rashid's reflection in the window.

'We have a grieving and very elderly King. Men opposed to Hanif becoming King will need to act quickly. And they will.'

Rashid's voice was like flint. 'All embassies will council caution during this interim period, remove what personnel isn't considered essential. God willing, it will be of short duration.'

'I'm so sorry.' She could think of nothing else to say. 'What will you do?'

'As soon as I know you are safe I will return to Samaah.'

'To Bahiyaa?'

'I need to be seen in the city. By being there I can instil confidence, minimise the consequences of the next few days.'

Dangerous things. He might even be killed. 'Ra—'

'Polly,' he interrupted her, 'there is something I need to tell you. Something you will discover as soon as you return home.'

His words seemed torn from him. Polly lost all desire to speak at all. There seemed a recklessness about Rashid now. A steely determination to do what had to be done and she had the strangest presentiment that what needed to be done was going to hurt.

'When I came to Shelton…'

Polly nodded because he paused.

'I did so because I wished to see your brother. Step-brother,' he corrected.

'A-about Golden Mile?'

'You knew?'

Polly flinched at the barklike tone of his question. 'I thought. Henry, Anthony's butler, said you were Golden Mile's secret purchaser. And I knew you were angry.'

'Do you know why?'

She shook her head. Weariness seemed to be seeping into her bones. It was over. All over. What she wanted was a quiet lie-down. Somewhere private where she could lick her wounds.

Instead she was going to have a long flight home. She would have to present a calm face to the world. Hide the heartbreak that was tearing her apart.

'Anthony isn't a man to do business with though. It seemed to make sense.'

'You are right.'

Polly looked up and caught the edge of Rashid's anger. It was gone in a moment, but she'd seen it all the same. Anthony had created a powerful enemy.

He seemed to brace himself to say what came next. His jaw was set firm, his eyes holding hers with a fierce determination. 'When I gave permission for this documentary to be made, I did so against my better judgement.'

'I know. You showed me the docu—'

'No, Polly. Yes, the documentary was a factor, but...' He turned away from her as though he thought it might be easier to speak if he couldn't see her face. 'I thought you might be involved.'

'In what?' Her voice was a husky whisper, her mind racing.

'Golden Mile is unable to sire anything.' He waited,

allowing her time to process what that meant. 'There were all the usual safeguards in place. All the usual checks: bloods, X-rays, airways, movement and sperm.'

She'd thought leaving Amrah, leaving Rashid, would have been painful enough; she hadn't anticipated anything like the agony she was now suffering. 'What did you think I was here to do?' she managed.

But she didn't need his answer. All those conversations. The times when he'd taken her to one side to talk to her. The interest he'd shown in her life. In Shelton. All were given a new perspective now.

'I thought you may have come to discredit Amrah. Discredit me. To find something that would hold me silent. Perhaps. I wasn't sure.'

The fact he'd not been sure didn't feel like much of a concession. Pain ripped through her. She'd been such a fool. A gullible, *stupid* fool.

'Why would I do that?'

'Because you love Shelton.' Rashid straightened his shoulders. 'And I'm going to take it.'

Shelton. This part was harder to understand. 'But surely…if Anthony has done something criminal…' *Surely he'd go to prison?* There had to be systems in place to protect against that kind of thing.

'I have offered him the option of repaying what he has stolen from me as I'd prefer it wasn't generally known my own agent, my own men, took bribes to cheat me.'

'He has no money. The more valuable paintings were sold months ago to private collectors. We only have copies. There's nothing—'

'He has Shelton.'

And then she understood.

It was like a dam bursting. For so long she'd lived in expectation that she wouldn't be able to keep the castle safe. She'd imagined this moment. The moment when she heard that everything Richard had strived for had been lost. But she had never imagined the words coming from the man she loved.

Tears welled up and fell down her cheeks unheeded. She scarcely knew they were there. All she felt was pain. Intense, cruel pain.

Rashid had never felt anything for her. He'd made her believe he cared, that he genuinely *liked* her. He'd made her feel special. He'd kissed her as though he wanted her with a passion that matched her own.

All lies.

'Polly, if there were another way I—'

'You'd let Anthony keep the castle?' She didn't believe that for one moment. Rashid was an implacable enemy and this touched his honour. She understood that.

'No. I can't do that.' He pulled a hand across the back of his neck. 'But I don't want this to hurt you or your mother. I will see the dowager duchess is—'

Polly stopped him. She didn't want Rashid feeling sorry for them, for her. If the only thing she could take away from Amrah was the tattered remains of her pride, so be it. 'I think you've got enough to be thinking about at the moment. I will see we're all right.'

'Polly!'

She stood up. 'It was all a lie, wasn't it?' she asked huskily. 'You. Me. Today.' Her voice broke on that last word. Their fabulous time in the desert. The sense of home.

'No, I—'

'Don't! Please don't.' She didn't want to hear the lies. No more. She didn't want him saying how much he'd enjoyed her company or any other spurious platitudes. The fact was he didn't love her. Nothing else really mattered but that.

She made an ineffectual swipe at her face. 'If I'm flying back to England tonight I'd better gather my things together.'

'Pol—'

'No!' Polly stood up, holding him off with her hand. 'No more. You will do what you need to do. I will take care of what I have to.'

Somehow, and she wasn't sure how, she managed to find her way out of the room. Karim looked up as she walked past but she kept on going, her back straight.

'Miss Anderson, allow me,' Karim said, coming to stand beside her and pushing the button that called the lift.

'Thank you.'

'I have already arranged for a helicopter to take you and your colleagues to the airport.'

'*Shukran.*' *Thank you.* Perhaps the last time she'd ever use those words because she couldn't ever imagine coming back to Amrah. Minty would find a replacement when the time came.

'*Afwan.* I will escort you myself. Shall we say within the hour?'

Polly nodded just as the lift doors closed.

'Polly, you need to sit down. Pace yourself.' The dowager duchess sat with a box of cutlery on her lap. 'The auction isn't for a couple of months yet.'

'I want this done.' *Done and finished.*

'Darling, Richard would have understood. None of this is of your making.'

Polly brushed a grubby hand across the side of her cheek. She knew that. It wasn't that that was eating away at her. The eight weeks since she'd left Amrah had passed so slowly and they'd been filled with difficult decisions.

The paintings they'd had copied quietly disappeared.

The 'Rembrandt' she took home, and had it propped up against her bedroom wall. Staff had been given their notice and had already begun to leave. Sotheby's auctioneers were coming next week to begin their valuations and it wanted only Anthony's word before the castle was officially on the market. Though he obviously had no intention of being in the country when he gave it.

Polly climbed the steps and held up two copper jelly moulds. 'I suppose these might be worth something.' She heard footsteps. 'Henry, have you—?'

'His Highness Prince Rashid bin Khalid bin Abdullah Al Baha, Your Grace.'

Polly looked round, almost falling from the steps she was standing on. She stood looking foolishly at Rashid, so handsome in a soft caramel linen suit.

Her mother turned her wheelchair around. 'I have heard a great deal about you. Since I'm sure you are aware my stepson left the castle weeks ago, I imagine you've come here to speak to my daughter. Henry,' she said, lifting up the cutlery box, 'put that on the table and then take me for a cup of tea in the housekeeper's room.'

Polly managed an inarticulate sound.

Her mother merely smiled and looked up at Rashid and Shelton's elderly butler. 'I am ready for a break. Polly is exhausting.'

'Have you come here to see Anthony? I'm afraid he isn't here. He—'

'No, I've come here to see you.'

She stepped down and placed the copper moulds down on the central kitchen table, then wiped her dusty hands down the sides of her jeans. 'We were going to open these old kitchens to the public some time next year. I'm not sure how much all this will realise, but something—'

'Polly—'

'Anthony had already gone by the time I got home.' She pulled the plastic clip from her hair and let it fall down around her shoulders. If she had to see Rashid again she wished she'd been dressed for it. Some sharp business suit. Make-up on. 'I'm doing what I can to raise your money but it takes time. I've spoken to Karim about it and he—'

'Yes, I know.' Rashid stepped forward and took hold of her hands. 'Polly, I have something to say—'

She gave a half-hiccup, half-cry and pulled her hands away. 'I don't like listening to the things you have to say.' Then, 'I'm sorry.' Polly turned back to face him. 'I do know none of this is your fault. It's Anthony's. I know. I—'

'But you are facing the consequences.'

'I'm mopping up the mess.' She took a shaky breath and attempted to change the subject. 'Prince Hanif was named as your grandfather's successor. You must be pleased.'

'Yes.'

Rashid's eyes didn't leave her face and Polly felt a compulsion to keep talking. 'And everyone seems to have accepted that. In fact, Minty was saying—'

'Polly, I have brought something to show you.' Rashid handed over an envelope.

She looked up at him. 'Wh—?'

'Please read it.'

A muscle pulsed in Rashid's cheek. He was nervous. Uncertain of her reaction. *And it mattered to him.* Polly looked down at the stiff envelope and carefully drew out the official-looking document inside.

He'd bought Shelton. But more than that. Much more.

Tears burnt the back of Polly's throat. So much so she found it difficult to get the words out. 'You've given it away? I don't—'

'I'm setting up a charitable trust to ensure Shelton's long-term future. I can stop this if you think it's wrong,' he said quickly. 'It will take time to finalise but this way Anthony and all future Dukes of Missenden will retain the right to live in an apartment at the castle. I know it's not the same…'

It was better than the same. Shelton would be safe. Its management would be in the hands of people who cared about it and who had the skills to protect it. But…it made no sense.

Rashid intended to allow Anthony the use of an apartment within his ancestral home without cost. The future Dukes of Missenden, too. For as long as the line continued unbroken. He was pouring a staggering amount of money into the trust fund to begin the most pressing conservation work.

Why? She knew how much Beaufort Stud Farm would realise and it wasn't enough to compensate him for this.

'Why would you do this for Anthony?'

'I want to do this for you,' he said quietly.

'But the money you spent on Golden Mile. You'll never—'

'The money was never important.' Rashid's hands found their way to his jacket pockets. 'What mattered was that Anthony should not be allowed to profit.'

'He does from this. He can still live at the castle. He—'

'And his son can, and his son's son. Isn't that what's important to you? What was important to your late stepfather?'

Polly nodded, tears threatening to choke her.

'And I found that what really mattered to me, beyond everything else, was you.'

Polly brought a hand up to cover her mouth, hoping that would somehow stop her from crying.

'I hurt you, and I'm sorry.' She shook her head but he continued anyway. 'I hurt you when all I want to do is make you happy. Keep you safe. Fill your life with adventure. Polly, I love you.'

It was like a dam bursting. Emotion flooded through her. It didn't matter she was standing in a dusty, unused Victorian kitchen. That she was in old jeans and an even older baggy shirt.

Rashid stepped forward and his thumbs smoothed away the tears on her cheeks, before he bent to kiss each eyelid.

'You need an Arab wife.'

'I need you,' he countered, his voice firm. 'I choose you. I want you to be the mother of my children. The woman who lives her life by my side. My equal. My heart.'

It was hard to think clearly when his hands were stroking her face, his eyes caressing her. 'My mother—'

'May well want to spend time in England, but I've put in ramps, lowered work surfaces...' He smiled. 'I choose you.'

Me. He wants me. Loves me.

'And once Hanif is secure we can even live in England if that's what you want. Polly, I have discovered my life is empty without you in it. I ache for you.'

As she ached for him.

'I can't settle to anything. I can't concentrate.'

Polly reached up and smoothed out the deep frown lines on his forehead. 'I do love you.'

His arms closed about her, fiercely possessive. Incredibly he hadn't been sure of her answer. She laughed up at him, letting all the love she felt for him show in her eyes. 'And I can love you in Amrah. But what I can't do is share you.'

Rashid placed a kiss beneath her ear and then another by her eye. 'Or I you. I will love you, and only you, until the day I die.'

His beautiful, sexy blue eyes held hers for a long, long moment until he was absolutely certain she believed him. And then he kissed her.

Really kissed her.

MILLS & BOON®
Pure reading pleasure™

NOVEMBER 2008 HARDBACK TITLES

ROMANCE

The Billionaire's Bride of Vengeance *Miranda Lee*	978 0 263 20382 0
The Santangeli Marriage *Sara Craven*	978 0 263 20383 7
The Spaniard's Virgin Housekeeper *Diana Hamilton*	978 0 263 20384 4
The Greek Tycoon's Reluctant Bride *Kate Hewitt*	978 0 263 20385 1
Innocent Mistress, Royal Wife *Robyn Donald*	978 0 263 20386 8
Taken for Revenge, Bedded for Pleasure *India Grey*	978 0 263 20387 5
The Billionaire Boss's Innocent Bride *Lindsay Armstrong*	978 0 263 20388 2
The Billionaire's Defiant Wife *Amanda Browning*	978 0 263 20389 9
Nanny to the Billionaire's Son *Barbara McMahon*	978 0 263 20390 5
Cinderella and the Sheikh *Natasha Oakley*	978 0 263 20391 2
Promoted: Secretary to Bride! *Jennie Adams*	978 0 263 20392 9
The Black Sheep's Proposal *Patricia Thayer*	978 0 263 20393 6
The Snow-Kissed Bride *Linda Goodnight*	978 0 263 20394 3
The Rancher's Runaway Princess *Donna Alward*	978 0 263 20395 0
The Greek Doctor's New-Year Baby *Kate Hardy*	978 0 263 20396 7
The Wife He's Been Waiting For *Dianne Drake*	978 0 263 20397 4

HISTORICAL

The Captain's Forbidden Miss *Margaret McPhee*	978 0 263 20216 8
The Earl and the Hoyden *Mary Nichols*	978 0 263 20217 5
From Governess to Society Bride *Helen Dickson*	978 0 263 20218 2

MEDICAL™

The Heart Surgeon's Secret Child *Meredith Webber*	978 0 263 19918 5
The Midwife's Little Miracle *Fiona McArthur*	978 0 263 19919 2
The Single Dad's New-Year Bride *Amy Andrews*	978 0 263 19920 8
Posh Doc Claims His Bride *Anne Fraser*	978 0 263 19921 5

1008 Gen Std I

MILLS & BOON®
Pure reading pleasure™

NOVEMBER 2008 LARGE PRINT TITLES

ROMANCE

Bought for Revenge, Bedded for Pleasure *Emma Darcy*	978 0 263 20090 4
Forbidden: The Billionaire's Virgin Princess *Lucy Monroe*	978 0 263 20091 1
The Greek Tycoon's Convenient Wife *Sharon Kendrick*	978 0 263 20092 8
The Marciano Love-Child *Melanie Milburne*	978 0 263 20093 5
Parents in Training *Barbara McMahon*	978 0 263 20094 2
Newlyweds of Convenience *Jessica Hart*	978 0 263 20095 9
The Desert Prince's Proposal *Nicola Marsh*	978 0 263 20096 6
Adopted: Outback Baby *Barbara Hannay*	978 0 263 20097 3

HISTORICAL

The Virtuous Courtesan *Mary Brendan*	978 0 263 20172 7
The Homeless Heiress *Anne Herries*	978 0 263 20173 4
Rebel Lady, Convenient Wife *June Francis*	978 0 263 20174 1

MEDICAL™

Nurse Bride, Bayside Wedding *Gill Sanderson*	978 0 263 19986 4
Billionaire Doctor, Ordinary Nurse *Carol Marinelli*	978 0 263 19987 1
The Sheikh Surgeon's Baby *Meredith Webber*	978 0 263 19988 8
The Outback Doctor's Surprise Bride *Amy Andrews*	978 0 263 19989 5
A Wedding at Limestone Coast *Lucy Clark*	978 0 263 19990 1
The Doctor's Meant-To-Be Marriage *Janice Lynn*	978 0 263 19991 8

MILLS & BOON®

Pure reading pleasure™

DECEMBER 2008 HARDBACK TITLES

ROMANCE

The Ruthless Magnate's Virgin Mistress	978 0 263 20398 1
Lynne Graham	
The Greek's Forced Bride *Michelle Reid*	978 0 263 20399 8
The Sheikh's Rebellious Mistress *Sandra Marton*	978 0 263 20400 1
The Prince's Waitress Wife *Sarah Morgan*	978 0 263 20401 8
Bought for the Sicilian Billionaire's Bed	978 0 263 20402 5
Sharon Kendrick	
Count Maxime's Virgin *Susan Stephens*	978 0 263 20403 2
The Italian's Ruthless Baby Bargain *Margaret Mayo*	978 0 263 20404 9
Valenti's One-Month Mistress *Sabrina Philips*	978 0 263 20405 6
The Australian's Society Bride *Margaret Way*	978 0 263 20406 3
The Royal Marriage Arrangement *Rebecca Winters*	978 0 263 20407 0
Two Little Miracles *Caroline Anderson*	978 0 263 20408 7
Manhattan Boss, Diamond Proposal *Trish Wylie*	978 0 263 20409 4
Her Valentine Blind Date *Raye Morgan*	978 0 263 20410 0
The Bridesmaid and the Billionaire *Shirley Jump*	978 0 263 20411 7
Children's Doctor, Society Bride *Joanna Neil*	978 0 263 20412 4
Outback Doctor, English Bride *Leah Martyn*	978 0 263 20413 1

HISTORICAL

Marrying the Mistress *Juliet Landon*	978 0 263 20219 9
To Deceive a Duke *Amanda McCabe*	978 0 263 20220 5
Knight of Grace *Sophia James*	978 0 263 20221 2

MEDICAL™

The Heart Surgeon's Baby Surprise	978 0 263 19922 2
Meredith Webber	
A Wife for the Baby Doctor *Josie Metcalfe*	978 0 263 19923 9
The Royal Doctor's Bride *Jessica Matthews*	978 0 263 19924 6
Surgeon Boss, Surprise Dad *Janice Lynn*	978 0 263 19925 3

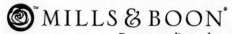

MILLS & BOON

Pure reading pleasure

DECEMBER 2008 LARGE PRINT TITLES

ROMANCE

Hired: The Sheikh's Secretary Mistress *Lucy Monroe*	978 0 263 20098 0
The Billionaire's Blackmailed Bride *Jacqueline Baird*	978 0 263 20099 7
The Sicilian's Innocent Mistress *Carole Mortimer*	978 0 263 20100 0
The Sheikh's Defiant Bride *Sandra Marton*	978 0 263 20101 7
Wanted: Royal Wife and Mother *Marion Lennox*	978 0 263 20102 4
The Boss's Unconventional Assistant *Jennie Adams*	978 0 263 20103 1
Inherited: Instant Family *Judy Christenberry*	978 0 263 20104 8
The Prince's Secret Bride *Raye Morgan*	978 0 263 20105 5

HISTORICAL

Miss Winthorpe's Elopement *Christine Merrill*	978 0 263 20175 8
The Rake's Unconventional Mistress *Juliet Landon*	978 0 263 20176 5
Rags-to-Riches Bride *Mary Nichols*	978 0 263 20177 2

MEDICAL™

Single Dad Seeks a Wife *Melanie Milburne*	978 0 263 19992 5
Her Four-Year Baby Secret *Alison Roberts*	978 0 263 19993 2
Country Doctor, Spring Bride *Abigail Gordon*	978 0 263 19994 9
Marrying the Runaway Bride *Jennifer Taylor*	978 0 263 19995 6
The Midwife's Baby *Fiona McArthur*	978 0 263 19996 3
The Fatherhood Miracle *Margaret Barker*	978 0 263 19997 0